The Time Capsule Murders:

BOOK ONE
Why Begins With W

Author Unknown

Presented by
Hamish De'Lamet & Chandral Ramon

PANGEA PRESS

Pangea.Press

Dedicated to our agent, Alphonse van Worden, Chandra's Dad Chuck, our mentor, Lee Schulte, the Good People of PANGEA, John Schulte, John Charles Besmehn & Cheryl Ann Wong. For Blythe Abigail Su-Ren Schulte—thanks for your inspiration and for coincidentally falling into our reading demographic!

Introduction

The box was metal, stainless steel, wrapped in plastic. The key was in the lock and turned fairly easily. The key's prongs were shaped like a "W," and there was a little tag on it that said, "Why Begins with W." The police here in Lynchburg were not interested when we called them. We explained that they should be interested in what the journals talked about, because of the crimes mentioned in them, but they just ignored us. So, we took the handwritten journals to a book agent, who's a colleague of Chandra's father. He asked us to transcribe them, as they were rather messy looking. There were side notes and scratched out phrases, irritating inserts, and commentary in the margins. So, we spent our summer and went through the laborious process of typing them into my computer. The agent decided to set us up with a small printer so we could just run with it. And now there's no looking back – only forward. We have many more pages to transcribe and try to make sense of – but we got as far as we got – and there's clearly a story here. And now you can read all about it. Maybe the crimes are real: if you have any information about whether or not these crimes were committed, and when they happened, please contact the publisher. Our agent came up with the name Time Capsule Murders, so we dedicate this first book to him. He claims the box we found was some sort of macabre time capsule, kept by a criminal who needed confession – as a ritual of his or her life. Our small town just doesn't go in for these kinds of stories. It cost us a summer of sorting it all out. If what happened in these journals is true, then, indeed, it was time well spent! If it's all fabrication, then the author should be grateful that we made heads and tails out of the occasionally illegible text!

But of course, the note in the box we found said everything happened someplace else a long time ago. Maybe that's why the Lynchburg police were not interested. Or maybe they just didn't believe us because we're young. And who knows if the writer was telling the whole truth, a version of the truth or, perhaps, was just mad? In fact, we don't even know who the author of these journals is. We're just finders, and now the keepers of what we think are a treasure of manuscript pages. We should probably someday tell the story of how we found all these writings, but it seems more important to us now to just get the facts out as we have found them. We're still rooting through many other pages and will make them available for publication, too, if there's an audience that wants to read them. One step at a time....

We're not sure if anyone else will share our enthusiasm and interest in these crime chronicles. But we feel a certain obligation to make them available to the world. Someone spent time writing all these entries. Certainly, the larger tragedy could be that these events are true. But we have no way of knowing, without the police. And they've made it clear they have no intentions of opening an investigation. Perhaps if enough people come forth and corroborate what we have documented the writer has written, they may change their minds. For now, one must read these entries as pure fiction. It's the only way we've been able to sleep at night.

— Hamish De'Lamet & Chandral Ramon Lynchburg, 2009

August 6

I am writing this because I am 14 years old, and have been thinking my life is over. My well-meaning parents are sending me to a regular high school. It's a big school: over 2,000 kids! But my parents think I need to be "socialized" more after years of home-schooling. I've actually been home-schooling myself for the last two years. My reading level is off the charts: nothing my parents have tried to teach me has been worthwhile. Well, it has, but I've just been reading through some college textbooks for a while, and they think I need some structure now and...

Blah-blah-blah! All of this sounds like the typical teenager who is arrogant, who has the whole world figured out, who suffers from *ennui* — a fancy French word that means a kind of boredom. You see? Just by using a fancy French word, and then explaining it to you, shows you how clever and arrogant I really am! Actually I'm never bored: my mind can always find something to entertain it, like watching the local cave boys in T-shirts and tennis shoes hopping around my neighborhood, video-gaming their way into jail because they're skipping school again. Sure, school is worthless for me, but not for them. They need it, because for six hours a day they won't be able to shoplift or dabble in drugs. They won't learn anything of course, but the adults want to keep crime low. That's why they need school. But I don't need it. Sure, arrogance again, but the truth has to be arrogant sometimes.

Anyway, it turns out my life is not over. It turns out this school might not be so bad after all, mainly because of the two deaths that happened there this week. Imagine that! You want to make school interesting? Here's how:

Have two people die in school under mysterious circumstances!

And I mean a real mind-messing mystery!

So you might think that these two deaths somehow involve me. Well, they do and they don't. I wasn't involved at first. The police thought they had things pretty well figured out. They don't of course, because they aren't dealing with typical criminals. Your average lawbreaker, like your average lawmaker, is an idiot, and so the police catch them quickly. The lawbreakers, I mean: on the other hand the police sometimes catch lawmakers too! That's what's wrong with America: we should just have the lawbreakers make the laws. It would be more efficient. But the crimes at school were not done by anyone average. How do I know this? Because I do. Trust me on this!

So that's why today somebody called on me to help, after the cases were closed. And the police closed them pretty quickly. Politics again, of course. The school board wanted a return to normalcy, just like Warren G. Harding, U.S. president after World War I and the inventor of the word "normalcy," and one of those lawmaker-lawbreakers I was talking about. Yes, I know, showing off again, but showing off is what brought me into the murders. In that first week the other kids knew how far above them I was, because I was flaunting my erudition (that means, showing off). And one of the kids came to me with secret information about the murder and the suicide, because she knew I had the intelligence to help her.

So now you probably want my name and so on. You won't get it. And I won't even reveal if I'm a boy or a girl. That would be telling. You figure it out: I'm telling you about a mystery after all.

August 15

Yes, nine days have gone by. I am taking my time, because I want to be sure about everything. Usually I have everything figured out pretty quickly, but with murder and suicide you always want to take your time. And I wanted to make sure that my informant, this girl who is scared and thinks I can save her from what she knows, isn't some loony-tune buffoon. She lacks confidence, and I don't trust people like that very much. If they lack confidence, then what they believe is fragile, and what she believed about the murder and suicide is not what the police believed after 3 days of investigating and then closing the case. People who lack confidence can be made to believe anything. So though intrigued by her offering, I still wanted to shop around a little bit longer.

Because they see me as strong, without sugarcoating or a luscious, whipped-cream filling in the center of my soul, these weak-willed people think they can leech their confidence from me. But you've got to know your limitations: that's the first rule of staying alive. And then you have to be able to look into the mirror every day and not shake your head, not laugh at what you see. Here's an example of where this girl's soul was one day, when she was talking to me: "I'm sure I must be a great disappointment to my mother. I've tried so hard to be good." No confident person ever says anything like that! This girl needs plastic surgery for her personality. And there's another thing clear to me: she has no idea what her limitations are, so she's almost a statistic waiting to happen.

Here's the set-up: August 3rd, day 3 of the school year; the school janitor is found dead by some seniors on the clean-up crew in the morning. He was still fairly fresh, dangling from a steam pipe down in the school's basement. The police estimated he had died only about half an hour before they arrived at the scene. Word spread about everything that was squeezed out of his body and dripping onto the floor: gruesome stuff. You don't need to know any more about it, because it doesn't matter in solving the case. How do I know? Like I said, trust me on this. What is interesting is that he used a chain to hang himself, and was not very far off the ground. A little step stool was found nearby. The newspaper said he strangled to death pretty slowly, because he had not been up high enough to snap his neck. You'd think a janitor, a handyman, might know things like that. Maybe he never watched one of those Westerns, where the hangman always has a nice big knot in the Devil's Necktie for the bad guy. If the janitor had a soul, it went gasping in slow motion into the next world.

What was interesting was the suicide note: it was typed on the janitor's computer and e-mailed to the principal. After he read it, he took the police upstairs to a storage room, where they found the body of a junior girl, named Aura, one of those names that parents sweat bone marrow over to make their child "special" or even "unique." So Aura was special for 17 years. School was canceled of course, and anyone who had already arrived was sent home as quickly as possible. I was one of them. No student came close to that storage room: everything was sealed off, so the police could remove Aura's body. As usual the television news had pictures of the body bags being loaded into ambulances. Then as usual they showed Aura's house, where all the idiot camera crews had waited and drooled for a picture of the parents, especially the mother. As is typical, the mother tried to escape, so the microphone morons attacked her with the ultimate microphone moron question: *"How do you feel?"* Then they spewed out the next stupidest question: *"Do you know why this happened?"* It would be nice to see someone whap and slap these T.V. reporters with their own microphones.

I had to wait, like everyone else, for the news media to assemble the story. And it was a nice, neat story, perfect for those who like their murder-suicide cases nice and neat. It seems that the janitor had fallen in love with Aura, the oldest story in the world. An old pathetic, pot-bellied poltroon starts fantasizing that a beautiful girl, 20 or 30 years younger, might actually become interested in him. The stalker finds ways to appear in her presence, maybe opens the door for her. As soon as she smiles at him, old P-Cubed thinks she is returning his sick, stalker love, when in reality she was just being kind and friendly. It was Aura's bad luck to be at school during the summer, practicing her various sports, jogging on the track early in the morning, and in the sights of old P-Cubed.

The newspaper version, longer and more detailed of course than anything on T.V., said there must have been an incident triggering the attack. Possibly she rejected him, when he finally pumped up enough nerve to talk to her. Possibly she even laughed at him. Possibly she just started screaming at him. The suicide note mentioned nothing directly. It had deeply stupid stuff about how Old P-Cubed "never meant to hurt her" – (what a cliché!) – but hurt her nonetheless. He "saw black," actually stated that he saw black – (another cliché!) – and when he came back to himself, Aura was dead.

Next came the weird Romeo and Juliet part, the Tristan and Isolde part. He wanted to follow her into death. That was the bizarre twist in the note. He hanged himself, not because he felt eternal guilt at killing the girl he loved. He hanged himself because he thought he could be with her in some afterlife. How sick is that? That was maybe not a cliché. Imagine: crossing over to the Other Side he looks around and there is Aura, happy to see the man who ended her obviously unhappy teenaged life. She embraces his paunchy ghostliness and they dance around the rainbow clouds like in bad drug-trip movies from the '60's. Aura backs away and looks at him very coyly. She's breathing heavily, and looks down at her long, white, silk dress, as her hand goes up to her neck and her fingers begin to move ambiguously. (A cliché, but it's the janitor's afterlife!) And right when old P-Cubed is starting to get really excited, a chain wraps around his neck and whips him down into a cauldron of Satan's best boiling oil: 100 billion years between oil changes. Fabulous.

By August 5th the police had everything figured out. Have you ever wondered about that expression, "figured out?" A figure is a symbol, a number, a geometric shape, an outline of something real. But what does the "out" really mean? I'm guessing it means you unravel the figure, stretch it "out" of shape, so that you can understand how it all fits back together. (Can you figure something up or down?) "Figure in" of course means to add in an extra number. See if you can figure that out!

And that's why the police did *not* have everything figured out! It's why they had everything figured wrong. They had no idea that, to find the true story about Aura and old P-Cubed, they should have figured somebody in. Her name was Anna.

August 16

Have you guessed that I back-date some of these entries? Pay attention, guys! I don't have time every day to continue the story. Today is not really the 16th, but I'll act like it is. Never ask a stranger the date, or eat spinach with him, unless he's Popeye. So yesterday Anna came up to me and said:

"I think you're...interesting, and smart, too, and I wanted to know, if you could help me."

Flattery. And so you think you might know something now about my gender? But you don't, because the way Anna said that first sentence was hesitant, stumbling even, without any hidden meaning. She could've been reading something off a menu. And "interesting" can always be a polite word for "boring" of course. And so now you think I've just revealed that I'm a girl, by denying that I'm a boy. Wrong again: I'm denying that you can ever know who I am!

But Anna at least knew me from my comments in our English class, which I made to keep myself entertained. Comments like: "How drunk was Hemingway when he wrote this nonsense?" I asked this with wide eyes and a completely earnest expression. Our befuddled teacher, Mr. Randolph, took my question seriously: "Oh, well, that's true. Hemingway had a drinking problem, we know that for sure. But I don't think it shows in the book at all." Another time I commented: "Why wasn't this book called *The One That Got Away* and put into *Fish and Stream* magazine?" Randolph the Red-Nosed Brainblear again was not sure about the intention behind my question, but gave me the benefit of the doubt. "Oh, well, that's true. It is a kind of fish story, but you must realize it's much more than just a fishing story!" Of course I realized that Hemingway thought he was writing some sort of great parable about life and death, except that he ended up writing crap. A third exchange occurred: "What does Hemingway imply at the end, when the tourists think the marlin's carcass is a shark's?" I answered: "That tourists are not ichthyologists." (That's a scientist who studies fish.) After that I knew that Mr. Randolph was not so dull that he would tolerate anything further. I wanted to debate the morality of murdering marlins, but that would've been just a little too much.

And I really want to be the anti-Hemingway. I most deeply desire to write ornately effusive, bombastically Baroque clauses, which twist and turn and swallow themselves like the Celtic serpents on the borders of medieval manuscripts. But I'm perverse. So I thought I'd annoy myself by limiting my natural style. For me verbosity is easy. Brevity will be my bugaboo, even though that fraud Hemingway practiced it toward the end of his life. And whose books are assigned in my first English class? Sure: the old fraud himself and his old fraud of a book *The Old Man and the Sea*. (Dreck: now there's a great word to use to describe most of Hemingway's manuscripts. It's a Yiddish word and it means quite simply, "excrement or worthless trash.") So why was *The Old Man and the Sea* required reading? Because the morons in my class can't read anything with words that have more than 5 letters. They won't read the book anyway, so what difference will it make? Why not assign one of the great books, like Jan Potocki's *The Manuscript Found at Saragossa,* instead of a boring monosyllabic fraud like Hemingway? The morons cannot read Potocki as easily as they cannot read Hemingway.

So probably because of these English class antics, or maybe just because of the word "ichthyologists," Anna decided I was interesting, smart, and able to help her. So I said:

"How?"

I said it with the same amount of neutrality. No surprise in my voice, no great interest in her need. I had no idea that she was about to make me more interesting than I already am. Whether or not she would make me smarter or dumber: now there's a hard question!

"I can't talk about it here."

We were in the middle of the cafeteria, full of the stench of fried Grade Z meat and roach residue. The roar of the greasy plates and the chattering of chained teeth made her request ridiculous: nobody could hear anything she might say to me. Maybe it would look suspicious somehow, or maybe I was still too new. Most of the kids knew each other from their grade schools. Maybe it was triple uncool to be seen with me for too long.

"Why?"

I can be like Hemingway when I want to!

"Too many people. I don't want anyone to overhear me."
"Okay. How about the library after school? That's alway deserted."

Which was true: why would high school students ever visit a library? Nothing but books there: a complete waste of time.

"Okay. Good idea. You know my name, right?"

"You...are the one they call...Anna." The slight hesitation was filled by my eyes looking directly into her face. My mother says I intimidate people by the way I can look at them. She says my great-grandfather had the same kind of eyes, the same look. (No, that is not a clue to my gender.) But there was no intimidation – I don't think – in my face, as I more carefully looked at her. I did intentionally use a stilted phrase right out of some B-level sci-fantasy yarn: You... are the one they call...Anna. I had to laugh at myself quietly. Anna was not one of the typical cows or sows that peopled our school. She was smart too, but not confident enough to let it shine forth. In English class she was completely silent. Or maybe she figured she would just keep her smarts to herself. I don't think boys were involved: boys really like girls who aren't very bright. (I won't bother explaining why.) Probably she was just shy.

But Anna smiled for a second when I said her name.

"Thanks. I'll see you then." Suddenly she looked nervous, directed her eyes down to the scuffs and debris on the cafeteria floor, and walked away. It almost seemed as if she realized that meeting me in the library would be extremely serious. At the time I had no idea what was happening in her head. But the mini-mystery made the boring afternoon classes less agonizing. Mysteries keep you awake. They give you strength.

So I went to Algebra, where more than half the class really has no strength at all to stay awake. All that grease from lunch clogs their brains and they fall asleep after about 5 minutes. Some come in and put sweaters or gym clothes on their desks as pillows for the moment when they will doze off: they don't want to bruise their pimples when their heads crash onto the desk. The ones who stay awake sit up in front with me. They're the ones who think Mr. Hudson might actually be able to teach them something. He is constantly looking at me, because I'm constantly smiling and nodding at him, even though I'm constantly thinking *What a jerk!* to myself. It's called conditioning in Psychology. You can condition teachers by smiling and nodding at them just like Pavlov got his dog to drool when he rang a bell. If you don't smile and nod, then they won't look at you. Actually, I think he's looking at me to make sure he's doing everything right. I'd respect him more, if he closed his Teacher's Manual, because I think he does know Math well enough to teach

Algebra. But he lacks confidence, and you know my opinion on that!

But today I wasn't thinking *What a jerk!* most of the time. I was wondering why Anna could not talk openly to me in the cafeteria, and what her problem might be. An itchy feeling in my left index finger told me she was not looking for aid in one of her subjects. The itchiness continued into the next class, American History, which is a fake, because it's actually Hitler History. In this first week the teacher gave us an overview of the "Big Topics" we would be covering this year. Except that this was a lie. *We* are not covering anything, because Coach Lewis so far spends most of the class giving speeches on Hitler and Nazism and why we should always be against any new Hitlers and Nazis. As he went through the course outline, he revealed his very unhealthy obsession with old Adolf. Columbus and the European colonization of America? Simply a warm-up for Coach Lewis to call it a Holocaust against the American Indians (or Native Americans, if you prefer). The American Revolution? Simply another warm-up for him to compare King George III to Hitler. The Civil War? Simply another warm-up to compare American slavery to the Holocaust. And I'm betting that in this class American History ended in 1945.

Anyway, today I put my itchy finger into the air several times to dispute a few things Coach Lewis was claiming. As he compared Cortez and the Spanish conquest of the Aztecs to the Nazi Blitzkrieg in Poland, my itchy finger went into the air.

"It isn't quite fair to compare those two things, Coach," I declared.

"Sure it is! There's some exact parallels: a handful of Spaniards with much better technology conquer a big, big area, just like the Germans and their Blitzkrieg with tanks and planes overwhelm the Polish cavalry and take over all of Poland."

"But the Nazis didn't take over all of Poland."

This caused even the sleepers to wake up: I was challenging the COACH! And it was starting to sound like I was a Nazi sympathizer, which I am not.

"Sure they did! September 1, 1939."

The Coach was very good with dates.

"Have you forgotten Stalin and the Russians invaded Poland at the same time?"

Whoops! Yes, in his enthusiasm to prevent Nazism from taking root in the newest generation of Americans, he had forgotten that. "Well okay, I mean the Germans took over most of it. Anyway...."

My itchy left index finger again went into the air. The Coach was now becoming agitated. All heads were swiveling back and forth between us. I couldn't help but think that most of the teens thought this was cool and exciting. At the very least, I was helping to make the class interesting!

"What now?"

"What I meant by saying 'it isn't fair to compare' was that you're comparing the Aztecs to Poland."

"Right! Both countries got taken over by invaders with better technology."

"Technology is irrelevant in these instances, isn't it." I didn't really state that like a question – I was being rhetorical!

There was oohing and ahhing at the word "irrelevant," possibly because I used a word with four syllables, possibly because of my implication, possibly because it sounded rhetorical!

"Look, you don't know what you're talking about."

"The Spaniards had help from other Indian tribes: those tribes hated the Aztecs because they were slaves, and because the Aztecs practiced human sacrifice and cannibalism. The Spaniards could never have conquered Mexico without help from other tribes. I read about it during the summer."

"Yeah, well, that's just one historian's opinion. Historians debate things like that back 'n' forth. Anyway...."

That itchy finger again went into the air!

"This ain't a debate!" said Coach Lewis, now with some impatient anger.

"I know. I want to tell you what was unfair. I didn't finish what I wanted to say."

"Five seconds."

"Poland wasn't a country with slaves and cannibalism. Mexico was: that's what's unfair."

"Yeah, well, I wasn't talkin' about that. I was talkin' about the technology of warfare."

"I know, and the comparison isn't right."

"That's just your opinion 'cause you've read one little book about it. Now I can't get into debates about every little thing. That's for the professional historians."

Coach Lewis at least admitted he was not a professional historian. That exchange was fun, and probably added to my reputation. But I'm not trying to get a reputation. I was just trying to kill some time. Who cares what these kids think? And you can tell that I don't really care what anybody thinks of me. I only care what I think. Arrogant little me coming through again. Of course I keep this to myself. I'm not nasty or arrogant to the other kids. Just here on paper, where it's okay to write my nasty and arrogant thoughts. I might consider myself better brained than they are, but I wouldn't insult them because of their genetics. That's just stupid: it's called bigotry. Coach Lewis can't really help that he's a coach first and a teacher of history second. I'm sure he'd rather have the cave-boys run scrimmage than debate the parallels of Nazism throughout history.

So there was one more class to suffer through: that's right! English, with Anna, Mr. Randolph, and Hemingway. Today we were supposed to discuss the symbolism of *The Old Man and the Sea*. This discussion unnerved Mr. Randolph a little: we are in a public high school, and this book, because of the fish, and the fisherman and so on, is easily connected to Christian ideas. Or even Jewish ones: Jonah and the whale from the Old Testament come to mind. To prevent anyone from thinking he might be promoting religion in any way, Mr. Randolph issued an uneasy statement at the beginning.

"Many people think Hemingway had Christian symbols in mind for this book. But I don't want to talk about them. That's a little too easy, a little too obvious. So let's...."

I raised my hand and interrupted him.

"We won't tell anyone, if you want to talk about religion," I said. "You know, the Bible can be read as literature too."

"Well, no, that's not a problem. I just think...."

"Is the marlin Jesus maybe, and that's how the Old Man finds religion at the end of his life? And the shark eating the marlin is the attack of evil."

"I said we're going to look at the book from a different angle."

"And when the tourists can't tell the marlin from the shark, that's modern relativism."

Mr. Randolph raised his hand and then pointed his finger at me. I stopped. You've got to know your limitations. And Mr. Randolph wasn't stupid about where I stood. So he rattled on about the symbolism of the conflicts of MAN VS. NATURE and MAN VS. HIMSELF to students who were only concerned about the symbolism of MAN VS. TIME as they yawned at the clock.

When the bell rang, I strolled toward the library. To be honest, a few kids were there, but mainly because their buses left later. Anna had stopped at her locker, and then she walked in. She went to an unoccupied table in the back, and after a long second I went toward her and stood between her and a bookcase full of encyclopedias.

"So," I said in a half whisper, "why do you need my help?" "'Cause you're smart, and I think you'll know what to do." "About what?"

"It's more about who."

I skipped the grammar lesson on "who" vs. "whom."

"Okay, so tell me."

I was expecting a sad tale about peer pressure, about being bullied, about a boy ignoring her, about parents ignoring her, about drugs or booze or a pet hamster. Instead she says:

"Do you remember the janitor?"

"Sure. Mr. Richard Laurenz, school janitor, stalker of young girls, murderer, and a suicide. Who cares about him? Richard Laurenz is dead."

"There's something wrong about the way he died, and I don't know what to do."

"There are all kinds of things wrong about *why* he died," I said.

Her eyes had a frightened look, which then changed to amazement.

"How would you know that?" she asked. "How could you know that?"

"Why not? He hanged himself because he stalked and killed a girl here in school. That's what's wrong about why he died."

"Oh. Okay. So that's what you meant."

"Now tell me what *you* meant."

"It's like, the worst secret ever, the most horrible thing you could ever imagine. I...I'm afraid of everything because of it."

"So what's this secret about? The janitor I'm guessing? And I don't want to guess what's going on in your head." Anna closed her eyes and whispered:

"He didn't commit suicide!"

It's hard to surprise me. When I said I didn't want to guess what was in her head, I was guessing about it anyway. I thought maybe she had also been stalked by Dick Laurenz, also known as old P-Cubed, and was now happy that he was dead, but also feeling guilty about feeling happy. Or that Aura Malper was her best friend, or her cousin, or her best friend's cousin, and that she was depressed about it, and maybe thinking of suicide herself. Teenagers can think odd thoughts. Clusters of suicides happen in schools sometimes. There was a whole series of articles once in the newspaper all about teen suicides – how they happen in patterns, kind of like when all those rich folk became poor on Black Tuesday in 1929 and started jumping out of the windows of their offices.

Another thought came to me. I kept it in the lower drawer of my memory for now. But now it was my turn to ask one of Anna's earlier questions.

"Okay, so how could *you* know that?"

"Because I saw it." She still had her eyes closed, so I said: "Look at me."

"Why?"

"Look at me." She opened her eyes and nervously moved them at angles. Only for a split second did they actually look into my eyes. "Look at me, and tell me exactly what you saw. What's the 'it' that you saw?"

"I can't."

"Anna, you're really frustrating me. I can't help you like this." She used a low-class curse word and started crying.

"I have to close my eyes, because if I keep them open, the whole thing happens again, right in front of me, if I talk about it."

"When have you ever talked about it?"

"I've never talked about it. You're the only one."

"Then how do you know you'll see the whole thing happen again?"

Anna composed herself, then wiped her nose.

"I don't know. It's just a feeling, a fear, and I don't want to test myself. I just know what'll happen if I keep my eyes open." She looked at me finally, right in the eyes. Anna has large brown eyes, with some green in the center.

"You are smart. I was right about you. I hope you can tell me what to do."

"I need to know what this 'it' thing is first."

"Can I close my eyes while I talk about it?"

I'm not so stubborn that everyone has to do everything my way.

I'm used to people ignoring my wishes most of the time. With her eyes open and looking at me she would reveal her confidence and her truthfulness. But, I had to compromise.

"Okay, go ahead and close your eyes. Just tell me what's going on. What did you see?"

"I saw how Mr. Laurenz died. It wasn't suicide. Somebody killed him. I couldn't tell who it was. And now I'm afraid I might be next."

August 17

I got tired of writing yesterday. That wasn't the end of the conversation. There was just a long pause where I nodded and thunked a few thoughts. The first thought I thunk: *I don't believe a word of this!* Remember that thought in the lower drawer of my memory? Here it is: maybe she was just testing me to see how smart I really was! Would I believe her lies? Would I swallow everything and beg for more? If I did, then she would run off to her friends and giggle and laugh at how stupid the new smart kid was. And so why did she have to close her eyes really? Because she was lying, that's why. The tears were nice: some good acting. And I liked the part about hallucinating the death of old Dick Laurenz. But I wasn't buying her mushrooms today. The whole thing was a cliché: and I always try to avoid clichés, unless I'm using them on purpose to make a point.

Still, I had to admit: what's the harm in going along with the fun? We can all pretend that there's a mystery surrounding the murder of Aura Malper and the suicide of Dick Laurenz. It'd be like little kids pretending to be characters in a T.V. show, or pretending to be Barbie or G.I. Joe. Maybe it would break up the boredom. And if, just by the tiniest if, she is telling the truth, then I did need to help her.

"Wow! So how did you happen to see all this?"

A few details here and there would expose her lies. She would contradict herself eventually, make a mistake somewhere, and then I would know that she was lying. So was she lying to test me really? Maybe not. Maybe she just wanted some attention. Maybe she was lonely and felt this would be the best way to make me a friend. Maybe she was insane. Not stark raving mad (that's a cliché), just a little mad, like some of those people in Hollywood and New York and Washington.

"I saw everything...sort of."

"What's that mean?"

"It means that I know Mr. Laurenz didn't commit suicide. I saw somebody kill him."

"And what did you do?"

"Nothing. I couldn't. I froze, and then..."

I was becoming halfway angry with this. Her acting was straight from second-rate movies, maybe even third-rate movies. So I thought I would provoke her as a test.

"And then what? You watch a murder and you don't call the police, you just freeze, you can't even run away screaming to spook the guy, you —"

"I *passed out!!!*" she yelled in despair, and started crying. "I know it was wrong, okay? I know I should've done something, I know, but I just passed out."

Now I wasn't so sure what was going on. The third-rate acting was now becoming worthy of Mr. Shakespeare. If this was a fake, it was a very real fake.

"The newspaper," I said with sympathy, "mentioned that Aura had come into school early to use the jogging track. Why were you here so early? You on a team too?"

Anna does not resemble the new classic high school female jock: she isn't small, but doesn't seem to have the hard muscle. She might be a third-stringer for the volleyball or softball teams. Cheerleader is also a pretty unlikely possibility. Water girl for the football team. Now that I could buy.

"I needed to get some homework done in the morning."

That crashed my computer. This is a public school. Nobody does homework! Some of the teachers don't even bother assigning it. And if they do, they really don't expect it to be done at home. That's why the last 20 minutes of some classes is "get started on our homework" time. There was something else wrong with this claim: it was also the first week of school. Was she really that concerned about grades already in a school where you get a C for smiling and not knifing the teacher? So I asked the silly question.

"Why?"

"Because I didn't get it done." Anna was still sniffling a little. "Which class?"

"What difference does that make?"

"I don't know. It might. I just want the whole story."

"Algebra."

If Anna is a good student, which is possible, then maybe she cares enough to want her Algebra homework done on time.

"When did you come into school?"

"You don't believe me, do you?"

Anna is much smarter than I thought. If I told her the truth, then the fun might be over. If I lied with big eyes that I bought everything she said, she'd probably know and get mad and the fun would still be over. So I lied with little eyes.

"I don't know if I believe you yet or not."

Anna sighed and looked away. She picked up her book-bag and stared at the floor.

"Then I guess you're not going to help me."

"When did I say that? All I said was, I'm not sure yet. Put yourself in my place. How do you think all this sounds?"

Anna pondered this for a few moments.

"Okay, yeah, I guess it sounds pretty unbelievable."

"So let's get down to what happened."

Anna swallowed carefully and nodded. Finally she gave me her story. She had come in around 7:00 in the morning. After about ten minutes she had to go to the bathroom, but the one by the library was still locked. Janitor Dick Laurenz hadn't unlocked it yet. So she went to another restroom, but it was locked too. She then decided to go downstairs to the janitor's office in the boiler room and ask him to unlock a bathroom somewhere. As she got closer to the janitor's area she heard the "weird noises." When she walked in she saw the office was empty, but kept hearing the noises.

The noises were coming from the chain being thrown over the pipe, and then more noises when the chain was being pulled to raise the janitor's body. This was happening on the other side of the large boiler, and when Anna glimpsed the figure holding onto the chain and the body dangling and struggling from it, that's when she ran away with her voice frozen in her throat; she fainted in the hall. When she woke up, she wasn't sure what had happened. But the worst thing was a voice in her head. She thought it could be a dream, but she thinks some more and decides it was the killer whispering in her ear, in her left ear, while she was unconscious: *Don't tell nobody nothin'! He had to die! And you don't need to know nothin'! Don't tell nobody!*

August 18

So I'm looking back at this conversation now today, and I'm wondering if Anna's story is legitimate. Because I'm supposed to believe that nobody notices her in the hall: the clean-up crew just happened *not* to walk the most direct route into the boiler area that day, so they didn't see Anna in the hall.

Worse, I'm supposed to believe that this intelligent girl is so terrorized by this phantom voice in her head, that she obeys its command not to tell anyone. She has the key to a murder-suicide, and the only person she tells...is me! Not the police. Not her parents. Not a sister or brother. She tells me, basically a stranger. This is a used car I'm not buyin'!

So back in the library I said:

"You're not telling me the truth."

Anna looked depressed and fearful. In spite of that I repeated: "You're not telling me the truth. I don't know what's really going on. I don't know why you picked me to hear all this, but you can just beat it now. See a shrink, get some help with that lying problem."

Anna did not move, but put her hands over her face and began sniffling again and breathing with big heaves. I don't know what it was about this new crying style, but I started to wonder what the options were.

First Option: everything she said is true. If her story's true, then the killer of Dick Laurenz is still out there, knows that he was seen – possibly – by Anna, and could be a real threat to her. Solution: go to the police. Except that Anna's story will re-open a closed case, will cause embarrassment to the police department for not doing a thorough job, and so they probably won't believe her. And if she does go to the police, it will hit the media: who can predict what happens then? And Anna has already shown that she is too afraid to tell the police.

Second Option: everything is false. There is no problem, if everything's false. Although in another view, there is a problem: Anna wants my attention for some reason, and this is her psychotic way of getting it. Solutions: do nothing, or go along with the gag to have some fun. Except that Anna didn't seem to be having too much fun right now.

There is still a Third Option: everything is partially true, and therefore partially false. But which parts? I had an "inkling," as my grandma would say, of what the true and false parts might be, but at the moment I'm still not sure. Anna looks real sympathetic right now, even miserable. What was really bothering me is that dead girl upstairs in the storage room: Anna's story had nothing to do with her. How did Aura Malper figure in? Solution: keep talking, and maybe she'll eventually reveal the truth.

"Okay, I'm sorry. I shouldn't be so skeptical, I guess. It's just the way I am."

"So you believe me now?" and she was regaining hope. "Let's say I don't disbelieve you."

"So... you think you can help me?"

"No. I think the police can."

"No! That's what he said not to do!"

"That isn't what you said. You said the voice whispered 'Don't tell nobody!' He said nothing about the police."

"But it's the same thing," she protested, and looked confused.

"Not quite. It's very general. I think a murderer would've used the word 'police.'"

Actually, I have no idea if that's right. It just felt right. And I think it is right. So then I said:

"Anyway, now that you've told me, you've defied his warning. You might as well tell the police now."

"No, I can't. It's bad enough that I decided to tell you."

"So what do you want me to do?"

"I thought you would know."

We were going in circles. There was only one solution.

"Okay. Here's what we do. We will have to open up your memory more, a lot more, so that we can track down the killer."

"We'll track him down?"

"That's the first problem. Are you sure the killer is a man?" "Well, sure, it has to be a man."

"No, it doesn't. Only if you're positive it was a man." Again I was waiting and looking for a sign that this was not a teenager's sick attempt for attention. Anna looked up at me for a long second with those big brown St. Bernard eyes.

"I think it had to be," she said. "Because who could surprise and strangle a big guy like the janitor? Especially with a chain?"

Elementary Physics would let almost anyone do it, I thought to myself. A pulley is one of the simple basic machines. That chain over the steam-pipe would let you pull more weight than you ever thought you could. Ask Archimedes or Isaac Newton.

"Okay. So are we looking for a man, or one of the bigger boys here?"

"What?"Anna looked confused, and seemed unable to comprehend that in fact one of the large alpha males grunting in the halls could be big enough to murder the janitor.

"It's obvious. If the police had not been so positive that it was suicide, they would've been interrogating every boy here within a certain size."

"Obvious? You really think that the murderer I saw is one of the boys? *And that he's still here?*" and she whispered the last question with her eyes wider than ever. I went back to thinking that she was a bad actress again, and that everything was a fake.

I stood up and put an end to the conversation.

"Yeah, that's definitely what I think. But I can't stay any longer. My parents'll be on me for being late for supper. Let me think about everything," I said. "I'll come up with a plan for you."

"It just can't be the police."

"That's the best plan. You've told me, and nobody has hit you with lightning or anything. You should tell them. And anyway, you shouldn't be afraid of a guy that uses double negatives."

"What?"

"Double negatives: 'don't tell nobody' really means 'tell somebody'! Like in Math: two negatives equal a positive."

"I never thought of that. See? That's the kind of stuff nobody else would think of." She wrapped her arms around her book-bag, and then said:

"I know you can help me."

So we left. Anna walked out of the library, while I wondered about her. Crazy girl or eyewitness to murder or something else? Whatever! School was becoming really interesting now!

August 19

Further thoughts about Anna: she has nice, St. Bernard eyes, but kept them shut or looking away from me most of the time we were talking. Did she really do that to stop the memory from coming back? Or to hide the truth? (And no, just because I like her eyes doesn't mean you know my gender now.) Or is she light sensitive? Or shy and embarrassed about being a coward? There! I said it! If everything she said is true, then she's a coward. And the reason she wants help now is guilt about the cowardice.

Anna: her name is a palindrome, spelled the same way backward and forward. Her name also has the same number of letters as Aura. I wonder if that means anything. But why would it? Although, now that I'm writing this, I want to kick myself for not asking Anna if she had any connection to Aura! Relative? Friend? Older sister of a friend? Her former babysitter? On the same team?

"No, I didn't know her," said Anna, and again she was looking away from me. We were in the library again before the first period.

"So here's what I've been thinking," I said slowly, even mysteriously, and now Anna had an eager expression. "Why does somebody string up the old janitor? What's the motive? The most likely motive...is revenge for him killing Aura."

I paused and waited for a reaction. But Anna just stared off into space. I continued:

"But there's a problem with that idea."

Now Anna twitched with surprise.

"Why's there a problem? Makes sense to me," she said.

"The problem is time. There's not much time for somebody to find Aura's body, somehow discover that the janitor killed her, and then hang the guy for revenge. Then afterward they write a phony suicide note off the top of their head, all inside of 30 minutes? Stretches believability. And the other thing is...the odds are in the janitor's favor."

"What odds? I don't get it."

"That nobody would find Aura's body: early in the morning hardly anybody's around. The odds are really against anybody seeing anything, you know?"

Anna simply nodded and looked at me. Two more things came to mind, but I didn't want to tell her yet. I had actually thought of one earlier. I wondered if the murderer of the janitor had also killed Aura. One thing the newspaper had reported was that according to the police Laurenz had not molested Aura. Because of the suicide note they believed in his obsession for her. The report mentioned "a lack of physical evidence" on both Aura's and the janitor's bodies: no scratches, no bites, no skin from the attacker under the fingernails, nothing biological definitely proving that old P-Cubed was her killer, except the confession in the suicide note. This began to bother me more: there was a great similarity between the two deaths.

This troubling idea led to a second troubling idea: if there was a third person, the murderer, why did they really kill Aura and the janitor? I needed more information. But the school was pretty weird ever since the murders. The kids weren't all right: they weren't doing much, weren't talking much. Absenteeism was up, and so things were pretty quiet. But counselors and school psychologists had offices full of kids traumatized by everything. Aura suddenly had as many as 57 "best friends" who were all weepy and suffering nightmares. There were even some clean-up-crew members who were upset by Mr. Laurenz' death. This seemed to show

— maybe — that a few kids thought someone else murdered Aura Malper. Would they have sympathy for the janitor if they believed he was the murderer?

So now I had to make a choice. Invade the Valley of the Blonde Junior Girls to find out more about Aura, or invade the French underground of the broom-pushers. For the first it would be possible only if I were a blonde junior girl myself. For the second I would need to be one of the student-council, service-type boys. And so now you are thinking you will finally find out whether I am a boy or a girl.

Let's say then that I have to admit that I am a girl. But I am neither blonde nor a junior, and both handicaps will probably prevent me from finding out much. If I admit to being a boy, similar handicaps – I'm a freshman, and not on the student council – will also prevent me from finding out much. Solution: gain the confidence of a blonde junior girl and of a work-crew boy to get the information. And then you will still need to guess my gender!

Which blonde junior girl and which work-crew boy? Solution: look for one who had younger brothers or sisters in the freshman class. A brother or sister could become my bridge to the information I needed from both groups. And then? Who knows? I would follow the information, follow the "leads" as they say in the police and detective shows. And where would I find a lead? At the garbage pit known as the school cafeteria!

"We need to keep our eyes and ears open," I said to Anna. "Especially around any of the older girls who knew Aura."

I told her I'd see her later. After snooping around the cafeteria I had a connection. It wasn't easy at first. I decided to try a random approach. Sitting down next to a skinny, hatchet-faced girl who was alone at a table and had a History book next to her tray, I started a conversation.

"You're in Hitler History with me, aren't you? Coach Lewis?"

She had long oily blonde hair, and a personality that screamed she would become an Ivy League yuppie lawyer arguing cases before the Supreme Court by age 30. Squinting at me the girl answered:

"Well, I've got Coach Lewis, but you're not in my class," and she turned away. I could see by her attitude that she meant that last part in two ways.

"A real waste of time, that class," I said, and received a hatchet- faced sniff as a reply. "The coach is a real moron. I've even caught him saying things that were downright wrong a couple times. And he won't admit it, if he's wrong."

The crickets replied, but not Miss Oily Blonde. She just finished her salad.

"But why should he?" I continued. "It doesn't matter if he's incompetent. He's protected by the union. The whole school system is a fraud. School systems stink from coast to coast and every American can smell them."

"Yeah, why should he admit anything, if he's a moron?" and she stood up and walked away. The girl was right, and I saw I needed to improve my powers of small talk. Next I tried talking to two boys who, I was positive, were freshmen. They were in my English class.

"Hey," said one of them, and he called my name. "You're good at wasting time in class. Really good!"

"Just boredom talking," I said modestly.

"Everybody hates that dumb book! English is such a waste anyway," said the other kid. He then added several low-class swear words to describe the experience of reading Hemingway. You can guess why he might have done this: if I'm a boy, he would be trying to impress me with his tough obscene talk. If I'm a girl, he would be trying to impress me with his tough obscene talk. (The game continues!)

"We should be reading something else, like murder mysteries or something," I said. "Of course, we already have a murder mystery."

"We do?" said the potty-mouth kid.

"Well, yeah, you know, the janitor and that girl, Aura Malper?" "Why's that a mystery?" said the first boy.

"You haven't heard all the rumors?" I asked. On the spur of the moment I decided to start at least one rumor. It struck me that this could end up being extremely stupid and dangerous. If there was a still a real murderer out there, this rumor could lead them back to me.

"The police think there's something wrong with the suicide part, that maybe it's a double homicide."

"I never heard that," said Mr. Toilet Tongue, and flushed a curse to impress me.

"Me either," said the other.

"Doesn't matter: that's the rumor."

"Where'd you hear it?"

Okay: if you're going to start a rumor, make it a good one!

"I overheard it in the main office, when the principal was on the phone."

Ollie Obscene offered another tiresome curse of amazement. "Wow!" said the other boy. "That means...," and his voice trailed off.

"That means...," I said, "the case isn't closed. It means...," and I began whispering, "that the real murderer is still out there. Maybe still here in the school."

"Cool!"

"You guys know anybody on the work-crew that found the janitor's body? Or did you know that girl?"

"Nah. Why would we?" asked Mr. Clean. "Just wondering."

"How much time you gonna try and waste in English tomorrow?" he asked.

"As much as possible."

"Cool!"

A dead end with dead heads. So I kept looking around for another victim to interrogate. Finally I had some luck with twins: don't get the wrong idea! They're a brother and sister. So I sat down by them. To start things off, I said:

"You guys hear anything about that murder?"

The direct approach: I had wasted enough time.

"Why would we tell you?" asked the sister.

"Why not? I'm a detective," and I said that last part with a big smile. They both laughed. I introduced myself. (No names: my secret identity remains secret, but don't worry. I'm thinking I'll tell you eventually.)

"No, really, I've just been hearing stuff, you know. Like, maybe the old janitor didn't really hang himself."

"Yeah, we've heard that too."

Amazing! I had just started that rumor less than 3 minutes before, and I know the deadheads were not talking to these twins. Solutions: somebody else started the same rumor earlier. Or...they were just saying this to be friendly and make conversation: not exactly telling a lie, just politeness. Or...somebody besides Anna knew the truth.

(The murderer, of course, knew the truth, but why would he/she start that rumor?)

"Where'd you hear it?" I asked.

"Some of Aura's friends, I think," said the girl. "I heard 'em talkin' 'bout it in the Bio lab. I went in early 'n' their class was just finishin' up. This one girl, she was just goin' on 'n' on 'bout it."

"About what?"

"You know, 'bout how Mr. Laurenz maybe was murdered." "This girl's name Anna?"

The easiest solution: who else would be talking about this? Who already had talked about it? Who had problems looking me in the eye while telling the story?

"Nah, well, I dunno."

"I think her name's Emma," said the brother.

This was getting weirder: did every girl in this school have a first name with 4 letters?

"You sure it isn't Anna?"

"Nah, I dunno, maybe. If you really wanna find out, she's in the Bio lab after school."

I did really "wanna" find out, even if it meant spending time in my most unfavorite place, a Bio lab. So I wandered mentally through the afternoon classes: Algezebra, Hitler History, and Heminglish. At least we're coming to the end of Heminglish: test tomorrow on *The Old Man and the Sea*. But who cares about that when you got a murder to solve?

There were 5 older students in the lab. You know the kind: sweaty SAT types, the ones who will argue with a teacher forever to scrape a minus-sign from an A. I hung around one of the lab tables for a few minutes and acted like I was interested in trays full of formaldehyded animal parts.

Now I'm not real short, so I could be mistaken for a junior or senior, although one with a very innocent face. So I decided again on the direct approach. One girl was peering deeply into a microscope. There was something "Emma-ish" about her. I walked over to her and whispered:

"Excuse me, are you Emma?"

Her response was to glare at me and growl a low-class curse. (How many times have I used the phrase "low-class curse" so far? Have you been keeping count? Pay attention! It's 3. And is there such a thing as a high-class curse?) Microscope Molly apparently did not want to be bothered.

So I tried another girl at the far end of the lab, who did not seem to have noticed the minor ruckus caused by Microscope Molly. She was standing by one of the sinks and unpacking a bag.

"Excuse me, but do you happen to be Emma?"

"You looking for Emma Risley?" and she shoved strands of brown hair off her forehead, as she focused on me through her small glasses.

"Yeah, somebody said she'd be here after school today."

"Yeah, she's usually here. You her lab partner or something?" "No, not that. I was just interested in something. Somebody said she was talking about...Aura...and the janitor."

"Everybody's talking 'bout that," and she shrugged.

"Well, I mean," and now I lowered my voice to affect a confidential tone, as if we were good friends sharing a secret, "that not everyone's saying the janitor was murdered like Emma did."

"Emma said that?"

"That's what I've heard, and so..."

"Why would Emma say something like that?"

"You're right!" I said. "Knowing Emma, why would she? Emma isn't that kind of person. That's why I wanted to hear from her own..."

"You're dead meat!" and she grabbed a dissecting kit as she angrily stared at me. I think I might've gulped accidentally.

"I'm Emma Risley, and I don't know you from this fetal pig!" and she reached into one of the deep, black sinks and produced a former porker. "Who are you and why're you lying about knowing me?" She plopped the carcass onto the tray, took out a scalpel, and proceeded to disembowel Old Porky with a great deal of relish, although barbecue sauce would've been more appropriate.

I introduced myself and tried to calm her down.

"Sorry about that. It's just that there was this rumor going around about how you said the janitor was murdered. That he didn't commit suicide."

"So what's it to you?" and she held up what might've been a kidney, placed it on a board, and cut it in half.

"I know somebody who saw something. Something that says you're right."

Emma put the scalpel down and took in my serious expression. "Who's the somebody and what's the something?"

"Promised not to tell. The first part at least."

"What is this, kindergarten? You got something to say, say it!" "The something is that the somebody witnessed the murder." Emma picked up the scalpel, and with an emphatic low-class curse, compared me to hamburger with an expired date again, if I dared to lie to her.

School was now really not boring!

"C'mon, you're not about to kill me or even stab me with that thing," I said.

"That's right," she said. "Too many witnesses."

"So, what's going on? My somebody knows Mr. Laurenz was murdered. How do you know?"

"I didn't until now. But I knew it had to be a phony suicide."

"Why?"

"Because he was my uncle."

August 20

So Emma Risley is the niece of Dick

Laurenz: that was unexpected! I told Emma how terrified my informant was, that she did not want the police involved, or anybody who would tell the police. Emma said she understood that, but wanted to meet Anna in person, so I had to arrange a meeting.

I called up Anna and explained what I did.

"I don't think this is smart," she said.

"Why? Emma's a junior. We need some extra eyes and ears, especially around the upper-classmen. And she believes in you." "I know. That's why I don't think this is smart."

"I don't get it."

"I thought you were smart."

So this was a test of some sort! It looked like I had to cram for it really quickly.

"You don't believe...that Emma could be the murderer?" "I don't know what I believe. But I don't like this." "Emma is *not* a murderer."

"We don't know what she is, or who she is."

"She's the janitor's niece."

"That's what she says. We need to get some proof that she's telling the truth."

Anna wouldn't compromise, so I had an idea: the Risley family should be mentioned in the obituary for Dick Laurenz. Find a copy of the newspaper at the library, photocopy the obituary, and that should prove to Anna that

Emma was okay. Except I discovered that there was no obituary because there was no funeral. Over two weeks had gone by, and no mention of a funeral for Dick Laurenz. Solution: he was buried with no funeral, and therefore no obituary. Second solution: he hasn't been buried yet. He's still cooling his heels and everything else in the morgue. And if that's true, it could only mean one thing. The police were not done with the body, because the case wasn't closed. And the case wasn't closed, because the police did not believe in the suicide explanation.

What were the police doing? Maybe they were hoping the killer would somehow get careless, if he thought the case was closed. The killer brags to someone, or lets half a bottle of whiskey whisper that something wicked his way came. Maybe they were following a suspect already and were waiting for more evidence. Like an eyewitness. Like Anna. If my line of thought was right, Anna really ought to tell the police her story.

So I explained this to Anna. So she says:

"I told you, I can't go to the police. He'll know, the murderer will know!"

This made no sense. People sometimes get locked inside their own brains. They can't escape their fantasy future, even when it's silly. They assume the future is one line: anyone who knows anything about Einstein knows that Modern Physics will tell you there is more than one pathway into the future, and do you know why? Because there is no future! The future is not waiting to happen to us: we create the future right now. And right now I wanted to create a future where Anna takes her story to the police!

"The murderer can't know what you're doing," I explained. "He'd have to be some sort of super human with mind-reading powers. Or have robot cameras secretly following you around. None of that's possible. It's all...just an irrational fear." I avoided using the words "stupid" or "silly" to her.

"You're not the one who had her ear whispered into!"

That was true and would seem to checkmate my efforts. Still, I've been known to be stubborner than cream cheese on rye bread after 3 days. My mom says that. I'm not an expert on cream cheese or rye bread or their aging.

"And have you had any second thoughts about that voice being real?"

"No."

"It could still have been a dream, you know?"

"You don't believe me, you really don't believe me." Anna sounded like she might start crying.

"Would I be talking to you and wasting my time, if I didn't believe you?"

Silence on the other end, and then: "I guess not."

"So will you agree to meet Emma, if I can find out for sure that the janitor was her uncle?"

She sighed, but then agreed. Next step: check out Emma's story. So who would know? Solution: ask someone on the work-crew. Probably one of them would know, especially if they were juniors or seniors. The next day I went in early to look for the broom-pushers. Some noise was coming from a bathroom, so I went in, expecting to find a broom-pusher. I found a few drug-pushers instead: deadheads hanging out in the bathroom. Who comes in early to suck drugs? The druggies looked at me without a lot of sympathy.

"Hey narc! Get out!" said one of them, and the other two yelled the most lowest-class curses I'd heard since I was at a hockey game. I hopped out of the restroom as fast as I could, and thought I was free. But the unholy three slapped the door open against the wall, apparently practicing what they wanted to do to me.

So are they 3 girls or 3 boys? Does it matter? I was in big-time trouble. Running up the steps, I thought I had to be able to outrun them, because they were on drugs. Except that some drugs could speed you up. A trashcan beckoned to me, but that never seems to work in the movies or on T.V. It's another cliché: it slows down the prey, and the hunters just jump over it. An open classroom? Ducking into a classroom would just trap me.

Finally I saw a broom-pusher down a hallway. I ran to him. "Help! Some deadhead Nazis are after me!"

He looked only mildly interested, but he did stop sweeping long enough to mumble:

"I hate deadhead Nazis."

The kid kept sweeping, but I decided to stop running and to stand my ground. If they were going to beat me up, at least I'd have a witness. And because they were deadhead bullies, a strong offense could make them back down. (I've had some Oriental martial arts courses: part of the home-schooling.) The broom-pusher glanced at me. As the deadheads charged down the hall, he stepped aside, as if he wanted to watch them catch me and then grind me up. But then suddenly he swung his broom and kneecapped all 3 of them. The biggest one he punched in the stomach with the broom, and I thought we were about to see what the brute had eaten for breakfast. The other two stood up, shaking at the knees, and wondered if they wanted to attack him or me. The biggest one rolled over and gasped out something about death. It wasn't very poetic or religious.

"What's going on down there?" a teacher shouted from the other end of the hall. The cavalry arrives late of course.

I hate clichés like that! But now it was okay. The two hobbled off, while the third one got up slowly and growled:

"This ain't over!"

"Shoo, before someone drops a house on you! And your little dog too!"

The deadhead had no idea what I was talking about, but the broom-pusher laughed. The teacher was getting closer, so I said:

"Thanks for the help. Don't worry. They're just bullies." I introduced myself and he replied that his name was Sam. To the teacher we explained that the 3 deadheads could be easily busted right now for drug possession. He did not seem surprised and went off in their direction while pulling out a walkie-talkie from his belt.

Sam could be somebody valuable for the investigation: strong silent type and all that. More important than that: he could show me the janitor's office area. If I wanted to do this investigation right, I'd have to examine the scene of the crime.

"You done sweeping?" I asked.

"Looks like it."

"Let's go down to the janitor's office. I want to see where they found his body."

"You some sort of crime junkie?"

"Maybe."

"That sounds mysterious."

"The word 'maybe' is always mysterious."

"Why?"

"Because it means two opposites could both be right."

"You sound smart."

"I think maybe I *am* smart."

"Maybe?"

"'Maybe' is also a sign of modesty," and I smiled with a modest shrug.

"Mysterious and modest, all at the same time. I think maybe you're not really smart."

"Why's that?"

"Because you had 3 deadhead Nazis chasing you at 7:15 in the morning."

"That was just bad luck. Intelligence had nothing to do with it. Intelligence especially has nothing to do with those deadheads. Of course, it could also be good luck, because now I know who you are."

"So maybe it was bad luck. And maybe it was good luck."

Sam was smart.

"Right, because now if I hang around the janitor's area for a few minutes, it'll look okay, because I'm with an official member of the work crew."

"Maybe you should tell me really why you want to snoop around downstairs."

"'Maybe'? I'll assume that's the polite 'maybe'."

"Assume away."

"Okay. Really. I just want to see the spot where he committed suicide. Curiosity."

Sam said nothing for a few steps. Then he stopped and leaned on his broom, while he examined me from head to toe. Thoughts were being debated between his ears. Finally he leaned toward me and said:

"Mr. Laurenz didn't commit suicide."

Another witness? Like Anna? How was this possible? And then I looked more carefully at Sam. He could easily be a member of the football team. His body had bigger muscles than most adult men. The oddest thought then struck me, that...maybe...I had blundered into a confession...from the one who had strung up Mr. Laurenz with that chain, the dark figure, the one who had whispered into Anna's ear!

"How do you know that?"

"I just do."

"You know a girl named Emma?"

"Emma Risley? Yeah. Why?"

"Was she related to Mr. Laurenz?"

"Yeah. He's her uncle. Or was. So what?"

"She doesn't believe the suicide story either."

"I know."

"Is that why you don't believe he committed suicide? Because of her?"

"No. Like I said, I just know he didn't commit suicide. And he didn't murder Aura Malper either." Sam paused and then said: "You a friend of Emma's?"

I recalled Emma using the phrase "dead meat" to me while she dissected a pig.

"Actually more of an acquaintance."

We were now in the basement at the janitor's office. There was the usual hissing and humming from boilers and pipes. I examined the pipes for a clue as to which one might have had the chain wrapped around it with the janitor's body.

"Were you one of the guys who found the body?"

I was maybe being too direct, too cold even. Sam suddenly looked down and stared at the floor. He sighed.

"It was terrible, the terriblest thing I ever saw."

My ears caught the word "terriblest" and I wondered about why he would break a rule about adjective formation, when he seemed fairly intelligent. But then he said:

"I never knew, none of us knew, what happened when somebody was hanged. It was...disgusting, and demeaning. One of the guys got sick right away, and said it was the terriblest thing he ever saw. I'll never forget that moment as long as I live. 'Terriblest' is something you'd hear down South, but at that moment...at that moment it was exactly the right word."

I was not sure what to say but knew what *not* to say. So I just kept quiet. Odd: there was something sort of holy about the conversation now. Because Sam had actually seen Death in its grossest form, he no longer seemed part of the teenager's high-school world of pot, pop, and pep rallies.

"Was it over here?" I asked softly, and then pointed to a spot on a pipe where the insulation around it was shredded. Sam nodded. I knelt down and began looking around for anything that the police might have missed, any kind of clue that might have rolled under or behind something nearby.

"What do you want here really?" asked Sam almost angrily.

I liked Sam, so I thought I'd take a chance again, like I had with Emma. Anna wouldn't like it, of course, but maybe she wouldn't need to know.

"I know someone who saw the murder."

Sam took a step backward.

"You...you can't know anybody who saw the murder!"

"Why not?" and my eyes must've been immense.

"Because I'm the only one who knows him!"

"Him? The witness I know is a girl!"

Sam took another step backward, and then the bell rang for the first period. We walked upstairs, and Sam whispered:

"We'll have to talk about this later. Which lunch period do you have?"

"Fourth. Freshmen and sophomores."

"Then meet me after school by Room 222."

Sam never showed up. I asked around, and somebody said he got sick in the middle of the day and went home. That made me nervous. Maybe something had gone wrong: and one main thought burned in me. Maybe his "witness" was actually the murderer.

August 21

A very sleepless night! Things were starting to come together too well and too dangerously. The only solution so far is that Sam's witness is the murderer: and if Sam told him that *I* knew a witness to the murder, then I could be in real danger. I guess I never realized how much jeopardy my life might be in by fooling around like a detective. Escaping boredom by investigating the suicide was one thing: being placed on a death-list was another! But all my restlessness was based on the idea that everything actually happened differently from the official version. My new friends and their imaginations might be keeping me up, instead of any real danger.

Today I had to get Anna to talk with Emma, and of course I had to find Sam. But Sam's name appeared on the absentee list. This meant that his parents must've called the main office to say he was sick. A silly, paranoid idea hit me: Sam was dead, killed and buried somewhere by the murderer, who then called the school to report Sam's absence. Yes, I kept telling myself: a silly, paranoid idea. After saying this a few more times I almost started to believe it. Almost.

But if I didn't catch Anna or Sam in the morning, I'd have to wait until lunch. So I'd have to suffer through the morning. The school has a 15-minute Homeroom period to open the day. This lets the administration take attendance, lets late students report, and lets students who care about grades to copy homework from stupid friends. Students who don't care about grades usually fall asleep within seconds. Others chug various kinds of high sugar and caffeine drinks to jolt their brains into consciousness. Some talk about their fantasies, movies, T.V. shows, songs, gossip about their friends and enemies, and so on.

First period is World Geography. It's supposed to teach us about other cultures on the planet, like where they are for one thing, and about current events. The illiterates in the class who can neither read a text nor a map are a majority. To boost their grades the teacher, Mr. Raymond Dunwoody, gives them A's if they bring in newspaper articles about a foreign country or culture that we've been studying.

Except he forgot that *they cannot read!* It means that too often they will show him something about California or Idaho, and he has to explain that those are not foreign countries. The kid then looks very confused. At such times I weep for America's future.

But today there's a new girl in the class: she stands at Mr. Dunwoody's desk and looks shy. He nods, tells her that yes, she's been expected, she's on his computer's list, and then he points to an open desk.

"Everybody! We have a new member: Lana Todd is a new student in our school."

Lana keeps her head down, embarrassed to be singled out. She's a bleached blonde, wearing typical clothes, blue jeans and so on. Some crinkles by her eyes make her look older, and you can tell they'll get worse and worse as time goes on.

Sure, I say to myself, her name just had to have 4 letters and end in A!

Biology is my second period class. I had spent so much time trying to find Anna or Emma after first period that I had to sneak in through the lab to avoid being marked tardy. Today the teacher is celebrating a rite of dissection - vivisection actually – with a goldfish as the sacrificial lamb, so to speak. We sit and watch the heart of the goldfish beat, along with the whole operation, on an overhead projector. The animal is immobilized, its beating heart ignorant that The Grim Reaper is on the other side of the projector. All for the education of young Americans who thought fish usually were square, breaded, and deep-fried.

Today Biology was a double period because of this lab showing us how to torture goldfish. Otherwise I would have Phys Ed, which is the ultimate farce. Over 40 boys chased around the perimeter of the gym for two minutes by a stoner from the '60's called Coach Eddy. He has a plastic baseball bat that he beats against his hand, and he threatens to hit the rears of the plumper kids if they don't hurry up. This is grotesque, of course, since he's the fattest one in the place. The rest of the time we stand around, shoot baskets, play wiffle-ball, or throw little footballs around, while Coach Eddy reads the newspaper or talks football with his brownies.

So I survive the morning. In the cafeteria I scan the faces for Anna, Emma, and Sam. I'm hoping that Sam maybe came in late, and was no longer sick at home. As I look around, suddenly standing next to me is the new girl from World Geography, Lana.

"Hi, remember me? I'm from your World Geography class." This did not seem to fit her shyness, but I just shrugged and said:

"Yeah, you're Lana."

"Do you sit anywhere...special?"

I knew what Lana was hinting at. The new kid didn't know where to sit or whom to ask for an invitation. So I said:

"Any place that's open. Over there?"

Now I take a closer look at Lana. She really doesn't look like a freshman.

"How old are you?"

"I'm, like, on the edge of 17," she said.

"You're a little bit older than me. What're you doing in a freshman World Geography class?"

"They say, like, I need it to graduate. Didn't have it in my other school. In Philadelphia."

"On the whole, I'd rather be in Philadelphia."

"Really? Why?" She seemed unable to believe this.

"Why? Isn't it obvious? Wouldn't you want to be back there in a big city instead of here?"

"No, never. Philadelphia, it's like, you know, dying. Actually I'd really rather be, like, in California."

Like, like, like: like the way she talked was really annoying. And here's what was especially nuts: it didn't seem to fit her personality. She looked smarter than some typical dumb blonde always stuttering out "like" and "you know" all the time. But I didn't want to waste my time with her. I had to scout around for Emma or Sam or Anna.

And then things became more interesting:

"So what's all this about those murders?" she asked.

Bells and whistles began a racket in my ears. Plural: murders!

She said "murders" plural. The official explanation was one murder, one suicide. How was it possible that so many kids would suddenly be coming straight to little old me with questions about the murders? Coincidences make me nervous. But maybe it was just what a new kid would say at a school where there had been a murder, or murders. Anyway, I decided to ignore the bells and whistles for now. Since I could not see Emma, Sam, or Anna anywhere, I just got in the food line. Lana followed me.

"Somebody, like, strangled a girl upstairs or something? And somebody else died?" she asked further.

"You don't know about the janitor?"

"Like, I told you already, I'm just in from Philadelphia."

"There was only one murder. The janitor hanged himself downstairs in the boiler room, after he killed the girl upstairs."

We were going past some gruesome gravy and yellowish mashed potatoes, which one of the old ladies was plopping onto plates. "Pretty awful!" she said.

"Cafeteria food always is."

"No, like, I was talking about the hanging!" and she rolled her eyes. Then she said:

"So, like, did you know this girl that got killed? And who hanged the janitor?"

"I told you: he hanged himself. Suicide."

"Oh yeah, right."

Something was not right with Lana, and the bells and whistles were making a new racket. I remembered from my Latin lessons at home that *lana* means "wool" in Latin, and I got the feeling she was trying to pull some sheepskin over my eyes. Why the dumb blonde act?

We were now passing by the desserts. The old woman in charge pushed a plate at us and said:

"These muffins each have at least 19 elderberries in them!"

We felt obligated to be impressed, and so we took one.

"I'll bet you've never heard that before in Philadelphia!" I said. "No, and what's an elderberry anyway?"

"A little dark berry, kind of purplish. People make wine out of it. Ever see an old movie called *Arsenic and Old Lace?*"

We sat down at the end of an empty table.

"Never heard of it."

"It has these two little old ladies, and they poison old guys with elderberry wine."

"You mean, like, elderberry wine is poisonous?"

"No, I mean, like, they put poison in the elderberry wine. Then their idiot nephew gets rid of the bodies." She didn't notice the mockery: or ignored it at least.

"Sounds like a Halloween horror movie or something."

"No, actually it's a comedy."

"A comedy about killing people? Like, that is just so awful." This conversation was making no sense. If she thinks an old comedy about murder is "like, so awful," then why was she interested in a real murder? Wouldn't that be even worse?

"So, like, what happened with this murder?"

"Nothing happened. Case closed."

"I don't, like, understand how it's closed."

"Here's how: Janitor kills good-looking junior girl, feels remorse, writes suicide note, then hangs self. Case closed."

"But, like, somebody told me that, like, you know, the case isn't closed at all."

"It's closed. Trust me." And I said "trust me" because I didn't trust her.

"But, like, so, why would they say that?"

"Because they are idiots."

"That is so mean!"

"They certainly are: trying to fool you like that."

"No, like, I mean, what you said was mean!" she sing-songed and rolled her eyes again.

"No, like, I mean, the truth is mean now and then." This was really starting to bore and irk me. Thank heavens Sam walked into the cafeteria at that moment.

"Sorry, I can't talk any more. I have to see somebody now," I said.

"Oh, okay, sure, uh, see ya 'round."

Sam looked pale and confused, as he stood near the door. I walked up to him fairly quickly.

"Hey Sam! Where've you been? I saw your name was on the absentee list."

"Everything's out of control. Everything."

"You mean...about the murder? What's happened?" "Somebody found out about you. I don't like it. Don't like it at all." "Who?"

"I got this note yesterday stuffed into my locker, right before lunch. It made me sick. That's why I went home early."

Sam handed me the note, which had very little writing. It was actually a drawing of the janitor hanging by the chain, except that the figure might not have been the janitor. It might have been Sam. Under the figure were some obscenities – very low-class ones – and the words "You're next!!!"

"I wouldn't worry about it," I said, full of bravado. "It's just those punks trying to act tough. We can take it to the principal: that teacher who saw them yesterday can back us up. They'll be expelled for making a death threat."

"No, *not* the principal. We can't show it to him!"

This reaction was much too fearful and even irrational. Sam began looking around as if invisible spies were everywhere, and were now zooming in with microphones to eavesdrop on our conversation.

"That kid I know, the witness?" whispered Sam. "He told me the principal murdered the janitor!"

August 23

I couldn't write anything yesterday, which was just fine, since I wanted to think about was happening, and what was not happening. What was not happening: simplifying everything. And so simplification needed to start happening! Like in Math, where equations are easier to solve if you simplify their parts, this murder – if there was a murder – had to be simplified, if I was going to solve it. And instead of getting simpler, my "equation" seemed to grow complexity like a crystal!

Sam was positive that the obscene note was directly related to my knowing about his witness. Simplified: no, it could not. It had to be from the deadheads, specifically the deadhead who left us with the words "This ain't over!" Solution: ignore this note.

Next problem, more difficult: two witnesses who do not know about the existence of the other. How was this possible? How did they see only the murder of the janitor without seeing each other? Solution: find two vantage points that can focus on the pipe and the murder area, but which are blocked somehow from seeing each other. Second solution: Sam's witness is mistaken, or even lying. Third solution: Anna is mistaken or lying too. Simplified solution: there was no murder of the janitor. The police are right, and the kids are wrong.

Next problem, even more difficult: explain Aura Malper's murder upstairs, especially if the janitor is innocent. Solution: the principal murdered Aura, and then the janitor. Exactly why the principal would have murdered two people in his own school within 30 minutes is still a mystery. Everything so far is centered on the janitor not committing suicide. Nothing leads to why Aura was killed. Second solution: Sam's witness is not lying, but just wrong. Somebody resembling the principal is the murderer, or even someone not resembling the principal. Eyewitnesses are not always right, and the police will tell you that several eyewitnesses will sometimes even contradict each other. Simplified solution: the police are right again. They are especially right because of a problem with the stories of Sam's witness and Anna. Something didn't add up: a cliché, but just wait!

Plan A: it was time to check the janitor's area in the basement again to find those two vantage points, if they existed. So I asked Sam to meet me later after school. He never showed up. I didn't like this habit: as bad as the habit of a 90 year-old nun, to use a saying from my grandfather. Sam's absence was making me nervous. Did he receive another threat or something?

Plan B: I found Anna instead and persuaded her to go back to the scene of the crime. It was high time for this, and would help me find that second spot where Sam's witness might have been standing. And it was time for an experiment in psychology.

I found two push-brooms in a storage room and handed one to Anna.

"What's this for?"

"We're going to clean up this school. Get rid of all the garbage and sweep it into the sewers where it belongs. Except that the sewers flow into the river where we get the water that we all drink."

"No, c'mon, why do I need a broom?"

"So if anybody sees us near the janitor's office, they'll think we're just part of the work crew."

We slowly entered the janitorial area without anyone noticing anything about us.

"I think I'm going to be sick!" Anna said as she looked away.

"Look at me," I said with some authority, and stared right into her pupils.

"What?" and she shook her head and closed her eyes.

"Look at me!"

"I can't do staring contests," and she turned red. "And what're you trying to do with this 'Look at me!' stuff?"

"It isn't a staring contest. Look at me."

Anna made a better attempt this time. But it didn't last long. The result was what I hoped for. She was distracted and didn't vomit. "Where were you, when you...saw it?"

Anna nodded to the left side of one of the boilers. Then she nodded to the door marked *Janitorial Services*.

"When I backed out, that's where I fell, here by the door." "I thought you said you fainted."

"What? Are you kidding? When you faint, you fall." "Think: were you still conscious when you were standing?"

"Well, yeah, I think."

"Where did you get hurt when you fell?"

"Uh, I didn't get hurt."

And that was a detail I had missed! I suppose it was not impossible for someone to fall in a faint and not have one cut or bruise. Not one cut or bruise anywhere. It might not mean anything, but I had missed it.

"Do you remember how you fell?"

"No, well, maybe, I don't know. What difference does it make? I want to go. I don't want to stay down here."

"Just a minute. I want you to think really carefully: did you see anyone else besides the murderer and the janitor?"

Anna closed her eyes again. She shook her head. "No. There was nobody around."

"Okay, so where did you faint?"

"Over here."

It was now time for the psychological experiment in memory. "Lie down on the floor, just like on the day of the murder."

I noticed that Anna curled her knees up underneath her body. That explained why she had no cuts or bruises: she must have slumped down slowly, bending at the knees while still partly conscious. And now, as she rolled onto her left side, the experiment brought out its first big problem.

"There's something wrong with this," I said.

"What?"

"You're not remembering things the way they were."

"How would you know?"

"Because of what you told me about the voice."

"What was that?"

"You said that the voice whispered into your left ear. Your left ear is listening to the linoleum right now."

Anna looked annoyed, and sourly rolled onto her right side. "There! Satisfied?"

"Only if that's really the way it was. Otherwise, no, I'm not satisfied at all. So, were you on your right side or your left side when the guy whispered in your ear?"

"I don't see what difference it makes."

"The difference is the truth versus fantasy."

"I'm not lying!"

"I know you're not. I'm looking for accuracy."

Anna rolled back over to her left side.

"Something's wrong," Anna mumbled, and then sat up. She sighed. "I don't know, I don't know what I remember. You've got me all confused now." She stood up and then kicked her book bag. "He whispered into my left ear! I know it! I can feel his breath on it!" She closed her eyes.

"But?" I knew something else was coming.

"But...I'm positive I was lying on my left side when I woke up! I know it!"

"Only one explanation: you rolled over."

"I don't remember that."

"It's the only solution. Were your eyes open or closed when you rolled over?"

Anna became tentative and looked very nervous. She looked away at the ceiling. Then she hid her face in her hands.

"Can you remember something else for me instead?" I asked.

"I don't know."

"It's simple. It'll help us find the killer. Look at me."

Anna stared at me.

"What?" and she seemed about ready to cry. I had to be sure about something.

"You know what the principal sounds like?"

"Yeah?"

"Would his voice sound like the voice whispering in your ear?" Anna suddenly widened her eyes and said:

"The principal? Mr. Kaplan? Gorgeous George? No, no way!" "I didn't think so. Just checking something to be sure."

And that was the main problem with Sam's witness. Mr. Gorgeous.

George Kaplan did not seem like the murderous type. But the other problem was all those double negatives. *Don't tell nobody! He had to die! And you don't need to know nothin'! Don't tell nobody!* Mr. Kaplan would never have used double negatives like that. He wears bow-ties, and people with bow-ties don't use double negatives.

There was the possibility that Mr. Double G Kaplan might have deliberately used double negatives to throw off suspicious people like me. That was a stretch maybe, but now Anna was sure that the voice in her ear did not match the principal's. The final possibility was that the principal used double negatives *and* disguised his voice to hide his identity. That was another stretch, and only complicated things: I wanted simplification!

You already know, however, that because the principal's voice did not match Anna's memory, I now had the definite problem of two witnesses with different stories. But now I had to push Anna's memory again.

"Okay, so you need to try to remember something else." "What?"

"The whisperer's face."

"I told you, I never saw him!"

"But now I'm wondering if maybe you did. Your eyes might've seen him when you rolled over. You already said there's something wrong with what you're remembering."

Anna's face was showing a stressful storm in her soul. She closed her eyes and shook her head, as if she were trying to fling a rotten apple of a thought into the garbage. Then she placed her hands over her face.

"No, no," she said. "I don't remember seeing his face."

But everything about Anna's reaction, everything in me, absolutely everything here said that she really did see the man's face! And everything also said that the experience was still so awful that she could not admit this memory back into her conscious mind. I could sense there was no use in pushing her. At this point in the investigation a tough-guy detective in the movies might smack Anna across the railroad tracks attached to her bicuspids, and force her to remember. But that would be a cliché. And I'm not a tough-guy detective. But don't think that's a clue to whether I'm a boy or a girl! I've just seen too many old movies. So we left.

Your sexless investigator finally had to get Emma and Anna together to talk. I told Anna that I had confirmed (from Sam) that Dick Laurenz was Emma's uncle, so she agreed to meet her. Maybe Anna would be able to see that face if Emma's forceful personality confronted her. As we walked out of the boiler room with our brooms, we were confronted by somebody, somebody boring and annoying.

"Oh!" said the somebody. "Like, what're you doing here?"

"Like, what're *you* doing here?" Mocking Lana could become a new hobby for me.

"I was just, you know, looking around my new school." Lana looked at Anna with 17,000 questions in her face.

"And we're working," I said wiggling my broom.

"Oh, like, well, yeah, sure."

"This is Anna," I said. "And this is Lana. She transferred into school a couple days ago."

"What grade are you in?" asked Anna, and I knew why she was frowning.

"I'm a junior. You?"

"I'm just a freshman."

"Like, that is so funny. All the freshmen say that."

"Say what?" asked Anna, still frowning.

"They all go, like, 'just': 'I'm just a freshman.' Like, it's just so weird. This is, you know, déjà vu all over again. I was, like, talking to this guy upstairs, and he goes, like, 'I'm just a freshman.' And I'm like: 'That is so weird.' And he's like: 'Why's that weird?' And I'm like: 'That's the third time I've heard that.' And then he goes: 'Heard what?' And I go: 'Just! Third time I've heard someone say 'I'm *just* a freshman.'"

"You've been talking to a lot of kids," I said.

"Well, yeah, like, I'm just getting acquainted, you know?" "Yeah, like, I know. Well, like, you know, we have to go clean up the school now," and I smiled maybe a little sarcastically.

"Hey! Is this where it happened?" and Lana pointed into the boiler room. "You know, that murder?"

"No, I told you, there was no murder: the janitor committed suicide." Anna's eyes became really big and her lips almost wanted to produce a sound. But she kept quiet.

"Oh yeah, right."

Talk about déjà vu! Lana either had a bad memory, or did not want to believe the suicide story. I also did not like the way Lana just happened to show up down here. Maybe she was just trying to find her niche in the school, or just, like, y' know, kind of like curious in a, y' know, sort of stupid, like, dumb blonde way. Or maybe Sam or Emma had somehow blabbed about me and the alternate theory about the demise of Mr. Laurenz.

We told Lana good-bye and went to the laboratory where Emma Risley usually could be found. She was working on the dissection of something cute and furry. Anna wrinkled her nose. I whispered a greeting to her and introduced Anna.

"So! Finally! So you know that my uncle was murdered?" asked Emma with her teeth clenched.

"Yes, I...I'm sorry," said Anna.

"Your friend here says you won't talk to the police."

"I can't."

"You know what the Marines say about that?"

"No?"

"They say that 'can't means won't!' And in the Marines you had better not say you won't do something!"

"I'm not stupid. I know you want me to talk to the police. It's, it's just impossible. The murderer said he'd know, said I can't tell anyone."

"You are stupid! And you're a ... coward!"

The three dots were not hesitation: they were filled in with extremely low-class curse words which even the Marines would not allow. Anna turned red. She was the kind of girl who cried when she got angry.

"You've got no right to talk to me like that," and she immediately began sobbing.

"Rights? Don't talk to me about rights! How about my family's right to the truth? You should see my mother, afraid to go out of the house, shivering in her bed and crying all day. Depressed because the whole town says her brother was a pervert and a murderer! What about her rights? And Aura's family? What about their right to know that the real murderer of their daughter *still hasn't been caught?*" and Emma was shouting the last words and turning redder than Anna.

"Now here's what's going to happen," and Emma returned to her growling whisper. "You're going to the police! And you're going to tell them exactly what you saw! And you're going to clear my family's name!"

"He'll kill me too!" wailed Anna. "It won't matter, because he'll know, he'll *know,* he'll find out, and he'll kill me too!"

This was not working out the way I had hoped! So I drew Emma over to a table.

"Your friend's an idiot!" she said.

"I've already tried to get her to tell everything to the police. She's got this block in her mind."

"Because she's a blockhead."

"I mean she's scared out of her mind. That's why she came to me, to us. She thinks the killer won't know anything, if she only lets us know."

"Yeah, sure! But the guy becomes psychic if she tells the police! I'll repeat: she's stupid and a coward on top of it!"

Suddenly the obvious solution came to me! The only solution to Anna's memory problem, which might also solve her fear problem! But now I needed to calm down Emma.

"Look, her fear just keeps her from remembering, and I don't think making her cry and insulting her is the answer."

"So what're you going to do? Hypnotize her or something?"

Actually I had just wondered about that: the night before I was in the library and found some books about hypnotism. Of course real hypnosis is nothing like you see in the movies or on television. Hypnotism involves more relaxation than putting a spell on somebody. So I said a tense, teeth-gritting good-bye to Emma, and then took Anna back upstairs.

"Where're we going?" she asked. "Upstairs to the library."

"Why?"

"Trust me: we need to go to the library."

"I don't know why I should do anything you say. You seem to be on her side," she said like the sourest of lemons.

"Because I'm the only person you got in this on your side," I said, making instant lemonade. We walked into the library, where some couches were located.

"Anna, I need you to lie down and close your eyes again!"

"Why?"

"Just close your eyes, please!"

"All right, all right!"

After a few moments she asked:

"What am I supposed to do? What's going on?"

"You're doing an experiment that will explain some things."

"We tried this 'close your eyes' stuff before, and it didn't work."

"It might work this time. (Long pause.) Now concentrate. (Long pause.) You're on the floor, and the murderer is coming up to you. (Even longer pause.) You're waking up and you roll over. (Extremely long pause.) Your eyes are halfway open. (Shorter pause.) And now you quickly have an image of this whisperer hissing into your ear."

Anna began nodding.

"So you did see him? Or her?" I asked.

"Yes."

"Are they wearing something unusual?"

"Yes!" Anna opened her eyes. "They're wearing a uniform!"

"Which explains why you won't go to the police," I said.

"It does?"

"The murderer," I said slowly, "might be a cop."

August 25

TWO days have passed and no Sam. His name was on the absentee list again, and so everything has stalled. I found his telephone number, but there was no answer, even though at times I got a busy signal. No answer, even at 10:00 at night. What sort of family did he have? "Weird" is the only answer that came to me.

Until I talked to Sam's witness I couldn't go any further. Anna's memory stopped with the glimpse of the uniform bending down to her and whispering its advice.

So I thought it was time to concentrate on the Aura Malper side of this story. I have already theorized that if Dick Laurenz was innocent, then Aura Malper's death had to be even more mysterious. And if a policeman was the murderer, why would he have killed Aura? Our school had two police guards patrolling the halls, like many American public schools. One of them obviously had to be the one whom Anna saw with the janitor's body. One of them obviously was the whisperer. Obviously!

Except that it wasn't obvious. It was still questionable what Anna remembered really. I was linking her unwillingness to go to the police with the memory of the person in a uniform. Maybe I was jumping to conclusions with something that only seemed logical. "Jumping to conclusions" is a cliché, of course, and I probably should have written "leaping with logic" or "sprinting with syllogisms" to avoid the cliché, but then I would just be showing off again, instead of "keeping it simple," another cliché of course. Was I keeping things simple now by suspecting one of the police guards?

The answer seemed to be negative. I knew what the guards looked like. The one guard was ancient and obese; the other was obese and ancient. They were walking grandfather clocks, counting the hours until they could finally retire. They barely had the energy to walk the halls: getting the energy to commit murder seemed way beyond them. Still, if Anna's memory was even partially correct, they should be my primary suspects, because they were the only ones wearing uniforms in the school. So there was only one solution: I would have to interrogate them...as a member of the press.

They passed the time and doughnuts and gas at a table in the cafeteria during the periods when there was no service for lunch. I forged a note to leave Phys Ed early, zipped down to the cafeteria, and found them chatting right where they always were.

"Excuse me," and they looked up in some surprise. "I'm writing a story for the school's newspaper about the Malper-Laurenz murder-suicide, and thought you might have a comment about the case."

"Why ain't you t' class?" asked the one.

"Murder-suicide kinda answers itself, don't it kid?" grunted the other.

Two more adults who prove the complete irrelevance of English classes!

"So you're positive there's nothing else going on?"

"Nah, goin' on like what?"

"Whaddaya want us t' say, kid? It's over. Move on," said the other one, and he put his face deeper into his coffee cup.

"Could I ask an investigative question?"

"What kinda question's that?" said the first one.

"Where were you two when the murder-suicide happened?" Officer Coffee Cup growled out something into his java that I couldn't quite understand, maybe a super-low-class, curse-filled insult. Then he finally spat out:

"Off-duty!"

"Hey! Take it easy! The kid's just saw too many T.V. shows."

I love things like "has saw"! It keeps English alive and developing, "don't it?" But he agreed: "It was all over by the time we got here, kid."

"So you didn't get involved with the investigation?"

"Nope. We gots other stuff t' do with in the mornin'."

"We're just guards, not detectives, 'n' that's it," said Officer Coffee Cup. He rose, but he definitely was no flower, and waddled over to the eternal coffee machine to add another layer of yellow stains to his teeth.

I had a choice about what to do next. One was to walk away and just assume they had nothing to say. But what fun would that be?

"So you don't believe the rumor going around that Mr. Laurenz was murdered?"

I did decide not to add "by a man in a uniform" yet, so I could watch their reaction to the word "rumor" first.

"You kids've saw too many T.V. shows," said Officer Grammar Cracker. "It was that janitor did the murderin' and the suicidin' all in one."

"Makes it all nice and neat."

"That's 'cause it is nice 'n' neat, y' know? Now y' kin put an end to the rumor with your newspaper story. It's official. Case closed."

Officer Coffee Cup came back and continued to torture the plastic chair. I think I deeply annoyed him for some reason, because he practically sneered at me, as if he wanted to roast me alive for his lunch.

"Were you friends with Dick Laurenz?" I rhymed.

"We talked now and then," said Officer Grammar Cracker.

"But you wouldn't say you were friends? You're probably the same age, might have some things in common."

"Nah, just small talk."

"And did you know who Aura Malper was?"

"That's enough o' this! Beat it, kid!" said Officer Coffee Cup before he attacked a Danish cherry pastry.

"Aw, it's okay. What's the harm in playin' detective?" said his partner.

"What's the use in it?"

"So did you know who she was?" I persisted.

"Nah, we don't know none o' you kids," and Officer Grammar

Cracker waved his hand as if keeping a gnat away.

There was nothing more here, except for Officer Coffee Cup's nasty reaction. I didn't expect either of them to confess everything to me suddenly, like in bad old movies or T.V. shows. "All right! All right! I did it! And I'm glad, I tell you! Glad!!!" It would be easy to figure Officer Coffee Cup's reaction as possible guilt, but that would be the wrong road to hitchhike on. I was missing something about the uniform, if Anna's image was correct.

The principal came to my mind again: his bow-tie and suit might be a kind of uniform, if you stretch the definition.

But nothing else about that odd theory from Sam's mysterious eyewitness fit. Who else would be in a uniform? Somebody from the band or one of the sports teams? But that was not quite the kind of uniform Anna thought she remembered.

I decided to go back to Emma Risley for information on Aura Malper. The whole case was lopsided and needed balance now. Of course, Emma has seemed unbalanced now and then, but I was hoping for a lead. Silence surrounded that part of the case, and the silence was speaking to me that something was wrong. So I thought Emma, because she was a junior, ought to know something about Aura.

"I don't know anything about Aura," said Emma. "Except that she's dead."

"You weren't in any of her classes or anything?"

"How many ways you want it? No, nein, nada! I didn't know her. It's a big school."

"Okay, okay. You know anyone who would know something about her?"

"I don't know. I'll have to ask around."

"Do that. Right now it's the only way to find out more about your uncle's death."

"My uncle's murder, not death, murder!"

"I know. I was trying to be polite. I'm on your side, remember?"

"What about that Anna?"

"What about her? She wants the murder solved too."

"She doesn't seem serious about it to me."

"Trust me: she's quite earnest. We're on your side."

"The only way I'll think you're earnest is if your scared stupid little friend goes to the police."

"I'm working on it. But if I can get some info about Aura Malper it could help. Have you heard anything, anything at all, besides the official story, which would connect your uncle to Aura?"

"No."

"That 'no' doesn't sound as 'no' as your earlier ones."

"Trust me: I'm quite earnest. The answer is no."

Emma went off to the blackboard jungle of junior English, the honors version, where she claimed they actually read a book with no pictures and more than 200 pages. And not by Hemingway: instead it was good old *Lord of the Flies* by William Golding, which will probably be assigned forever in high school English classes because 1. it shows average teenaged boys becoming the average chimpanzees they really are, and 2. it shows that our civilization is a fraud, and bad news sells. Would you read a book about how our civilization is doing just fine? School teachers - in public schools especially - view America and our civilization as a crumbling fraud, like the school system, so Golding's negative vision fits in just fine. If it has the stench of decay and death, then the teachers love it.

On the other hand a stench can be annoying: Inspiration comes from annoyance. Satisfied people don't create anything. They don't write journals like this out of satisfaction. Dissatisfaction is the wheel of human progress. Read any history book and you'll see I'm right. But dissatisfaction can also be the wheel of regress! And right now I was not sure if this case was progressing or regressing.

Until Sam showed up in the hall a few minutes after Emma left and said:

"I'm sure glad I found you!"

"Sam! What's been going on? You're here for a day or two and then you leave me...wondering." I almost said "you leave me hanging" and was able to change direction.

"I've been home because of some problems," he said vaguely. "When's your next class?"

"Twenty minutes. I'm skipping Phys Ed right now, so I can work on the case. I talked to the doughnut cops and to Emma Risley. So what's up?"

"I got another death threat."

"I told you it's probably from the deadhead. It's all foam. Don't pay any attention to it."

"This one's different."

"How?"

Sam reached into his pocket and unfolded an unlined piece of paper. I frowned at first when I scanned it: "Your next!!!" (with the wrong word for "you're") was written in blue ink. There was no drawing.

"Did you bring the first one?" I asked. Sam nodded and pulled it out as well.

"Different handwriting and spelling," I shrugged. "Same source though: our deadhead just leaned on one of the other deadhead.

Nazis to write a threat to you now. I'd say it has nothing to do with the case."

"How do you know that? You can't know that."

"I know it because if you're right about where you were, and about your secret witness, then this can't have anything to do with Mr. Laurenz or Aura Malper."

Sam had a painful, thoughtful look on his face. Three large creases rippled across his forehead, which some oily black curls framed on three sides. He squinted and looked away, as if some spearing thought had pierced his eyes.

"You're really smart," he said.

"I hope you like that in your freshmen acquaintances."

"I like it, so far. And, well, tell me again: you're positive this is nothing to worry about."

"It's nothing to worry about. You can take care of those punks, right?"

"What about you? You're not as big as I am. If they come after you, alone, you'd be in trouble."

"You forgot: I've had some martial arts training."

"You sound confident too. Smart, confident, got everything figured out."

"No," I smiled, "not everything! Like this murder-suicide: I don't have that figured out yet."

"Well, I mean, you sound like you've got things under control."

"I give that impression at least!" and I smiled again. Sam was thinking of something behind this boring conversation. He was on auto-pilot. So I paused a moment and then said: "And what about you? You have things under control, right?"

Sam shrugged. A shrug in this case meant no. And watching him more carefully now, I saw in his drooping eyes something tired.

"Sam, what's wrong? What's been happening during these disappearing acts?"

"Not much."

My memory reached back into a textbook I read for my mother's Summer Psychology Course, and I began to wonder if Sam was depressed. Suddenly it struck me that he could be suffering from the trauma of seeing Mr. Laurenz swinging from that pipe. Images from a bad experience won't leave your mind, and people then sometimes begin to have all kinds of mental and physical problems. So I asked Sam:

"Have you had trouble sleeping because of this?"

Sam nodded at first, but then just shrugged and said:

"Well, maybe, I don't know."

He meant yes, but would not admit it. So I returned to the main point.

"So when can I talk to this witness of yours? It seems every time we're supposed to plan to get together with him, you disappear." Sam just shrugged again and said nothing.

"Does Emma Risley know about him?" I asked.

"Why?"

"Because if she does, she'll want him to take his story to the police, to clear her uncle's name. She's after my witness to do that."

"No, she doesn't know about him."

"I didn't think so. Now look, there are some real problems here. I don't think your witness is right about the principal being the murderer," and I explained how the contradictions were piling up. "So right now, out with it: who's the witness?"

"I can't tell you. Not just yet," and Sam seemed very upset.

"That's because you're lying!" and I decided to push Sam in spite of everything. "There is no witness! And you were never around the body. You never saw Mr. Laurenz at all! You've made everything up just to get some attention, so you can go to counselors and get out of class and take some days off and have everybody feel sorry for you that you had to be one of the people who saw his body."

"I was there with the other guys! We all saw him!"

"No, you saw nothing. You're just after some attention," and I spoke with a combination of pity and sarcasm.

"You don't know! You don't know what I saw! I was there! I'm telling the truth!"

"But not about this friend-witness who walked in earlier."

"Yes I am!"

"Then that's because you're the witness!"

The only solution was the oldest cliché in the book: a kid goes to an adult and says he has "this friend" with a problem, and wants to know how to help him, and of course the whole time "this friend" doesn't exist. The kid has the problem, not his imaginary friend.

Sam's mouth didn't quite close, and he seemed stupid suddenly. The bell rang for the next class, and he nearly ran away down the hall.

September 4

Labor Day vacation is over: a 3-day weekend spent dealing with chicks, hicks, and dictatorial parents.

My parents normally give me a great amount of freedom, because they trust me, and because they think I'm intelligent enough to behave, which is why they trust me. I don't want to imply that dumb kids can't be trusted, since intelligence and proper behavior don't always go together. You might not believe it, but smart kids are very capable of doing really dumb things. I have loads of examples, like Microscope Molly, who turned out to be a sophomore in that junior Biology class with Emma Risley. Smart girl, right? So I thought, until I saw her puffing away on a tobacco tube later in a parking lot. Or take the junior boy in 2 senior college-level classes: take him especially to a psychiatrist, because the idiot (the junior, not the psychiatrist) was found in an upstairs bathroom doing some very interesting exercises with a freshman girl. These exercises made the poor girl sound like a squirrel in a barrel of Brazil nuts, and of course a teacher came in to see what the strange noises were about. So, smart kids can do stupid stuff.

Anyway, on Saturday, right when I wanted to pursue a lead, my parents insisted that I go with them to visit my father's crazy twin cousins. For two years I had avoided visiting them, but my luck was on vacation suddenly. So I wasted a whole day listening to bad country music, which is probably redundant, and to conversations about beauticians, fry cooks, and other fine members of America who think a T.V. game show like *Jackpot Bowling* meets the definition for high culture. Except that it was not quite wasted: it turned out that my one cousin, Martika, attended my high school, and was a junior! This is what I get for not paying attention to family news.

So after acting surprised that we had not yet crossed paths at school, which was not quite a real act, because it is a big school and I had no idea what Martika looked like these days, I got right to the throat of the case: Did she know anything about Aura Malper?

"Yeah, she's dead," said Martika, and thought this was funny enough to laugh at, which allowed me to notice her teeth. They were slightly crooked, but because of other things, like her ability to walk very upright, a certain kind of boy (droopy eyes, greasy hair, 90 I.Q.) would probably find Martika attractive.

"Ever talk to her?" I asked.

"Yeah, sure. Now and then. We were kind of friends."

"What'd you talk about?"

"Stuff, you know, boys, and stuff. She had a pretty heavy thing going, you know, with this one guy. But then they broke up. That was back in the spring. She wasn't going with anybody since then. Too bad for her: he's a pretty cool dude."

"Who is he? Is he still in the school?"

"Steve, Steve Cadosia. Yeah, sure, he's still in school. Why wouldn't he be?"

"Maybe because his former girlfriend's body was found there." "Oh, yeah, okay, I can see that."

"So how's he been since she's died?"

"I guess he's been pretty torn up. Like the rest of us. That first week was really rough. Wouldn't you be, if you'd been her friend?" "Sure. So do you, does anybody you know, have any doubts about the janitor murdering her?"

"Well, maybe, but it doesn't make any sense," and Martika wrinkled her nose and shook her head at the thought, as if she were smelling cabbage cooking somewhere.

"Tell me. Maybe I can figure it out."

"You're a big expert on everything, huh Cuz?"

"No, not everything, but I'm working on it. So what've you heard?"

"Steve said he had these poems that Aura wrote. Death poems.

He said they're, like, pretty Goth, you know? And a couple of 'em... well, it was just weird. A couple of 'em talked about suicide."

"Yeah, so? Sounds like typical Goth stuff, if she was into that kind of thing."

"Yeah, well, Aura really wasn't, but, well, anyway, two of the poems talked about suffocating yourself in a plastic bag, you know, pulling a rope around your neck with a plastic bag on your head and passing out and then you'd suffocate and die."

I made a mental note to check my mother's psychology books about things like this.

"I can think of better ways of committing suicide," I said. "But was Aura found with a plastic bag around her head? The news reports didn't have anything about that."

"Well, they said she was strangled at least."

I nodded and thought back to everything that was reported. The news reported that she was strangled, but Martika was right: nothing was mentioned about *how*. Whether Mr. Laurenz had used his hands, a cord, or a rope was a detail that was missing. And nothing in the reports mentioned another plastic bag over her head. Still, this was interesting, an interesting coincidence.

I walked around Martika's room and thoughts began to swirl around my head. Coincidences like this weren't impossible. I noticed her swimsuit and cap lying on the bed: she was a member of the school's swim team. Then I happened to notice an unusual collection on one of her shelves.

"What's with this stuff?" I asked and pointed to a collection of old-fashioned toy soldiers. They were painted metal and represented various eras of warfare. "Not the typical things to find in a girl's room. Where's the teddy bear collection?"

"Packed away," she said, not picking up my teasing tone. "I kind of got interested in it when I did a project on the Civil War." She went over to her closet and brought out a camouflage uniform. "I even joined junior ROTC."

"Junior ROTC," I repeated. I had not heard anything about that, but it is a big school. "So our school has junior ROTC, and you're a member? Are there many girls in it?"

"No, but still there's some, and it's a good way to pay for college."

"You can shoot guns and all that?"

"Yeah, sure. I went through a summer boot camp and everything. Kind of hard, but kind of fun."

"And what happens if there's a war?"

"A war where? The Russians aren't a problem, and we've got nukes anyway. Chances are I'll never have to do anything dangerous, even if something does happen. I'd be working at a computer or something. Anyway, like I said, free college!"

"You're allowed to wear this at school?" and I pointed to the camouflage outfit.

"Yeah, some days we have to because we have drills and inspection and stuff."

"Do you remember if anybody wore this on the day the murders were discovered?"

"What difference does it make?"

"Just tell me. Just interested."

"Well, yeah, that was a day when we were supposed to wear our fatigues. But what difference does it make?"

"Like I said, just interested. And this Steve, the ex-boyfriend: is he in JROTC?"

"Yeah, he is. Now what's goin' on?"

My swirling thoughts from earlier all came together, like puzzle parts moving around and suddenly forming a picture. Steve Cadosia was wearing a camouflage outfit on that murderous day: and Anna had a memory that the whisperer, the murderer in her ear, *was wearing a uniform!*

Confession, they say, is good for the soul, if you believe in stuff like that. I'm not so sure, but of course that's just the way I am: skeptical, mocking, never really serious, or at least never really serious most of the time. Now I was really serious, and here's my confession: at this moment I began to believe that maybe (see, skeptical again!) the police were wrong! Up until now I will admit that I thought everything was probably just kids being full of rumors and hysteria and paranoia. Like I said, it was a fun way to endure the boring classes at school. Passing the time solving a crime's like making a rhyme about a mime: it was just something to do.

But now I actually began to wonder about Steve Cadosia, and why he might have killed Mr. Laurenz and faked the suicide. I actually began to wonder again if a murderer was walking through the halls of our school. I actually began to wonder again if this fun could become dangerous.

"Nothing," I shrugged.

"There's somethin' goin' on!" insisted Martika. "What is it?" and she suddenly seemed odd.

"Nothing."

"Nothing means something."

"That's impossible, and you know it."

"What I know is that you've been acting like a narc in the last few minutes with all your questions. You know something about Aura," and Martika began shaking. Perhaps Aura was a better friend than she was admitting.

"I really don't know anything except what I read in the newspaper and heard on the news." The word "really" was really a mistake there.

"So 'really don't know anything' means that there *is* something else goin' on!" and she became very angry for some reason.

"Hey, back off and cool down! For the last time, there's nothing going on! Really means exactly that: in reality."

"Bratty freshman playing with words now instead of blocks: you might think you're smart, but you're not!"

Martika's hostility made no sense, really! The only explanation was that she had been close to Aura. So I tried a soft approach.

"Sorry if it seemed like I was some sort of sicko asking about Aura. A murder doesn't happen every day in a school. Or a suicide. It must've been painful for you, when she was found dead."

"Painful," Martika repeated. "Yeah, Aura dead: that was painful," and she spaced out, a total zombie suddenly. Then she said: "You think it won't hurt, because it isn't you, and you're glad to be alive, secretly everybody's glad that *she's* the one that's dead, and not them. Everybody's thinking the same thing. But later, your mind tries to block everything out, everything goes black, so you won't feel bad, so you can shut out anything painful. In the end...only emptiness remains. It replaces all the pain. And then the emptiness is worse than the pain, because at least you know you're alive when you're in pain. When you're empty, you might as well be dead."

Martika at this point seemed angry, which did not seem to fit what she was talking about. Her short brown hair was electrified with static, and her dark eyes narrowed into squinting slits. She was gritting those slightly crooked teeth as she stood up, her wide shoulders showing the result of the hours of swimming practice.

I decided not to say anything more. Martika was in a fairly dark place right now, and I needed to turn on some light. So I suggested we go outside to the rest of the relatives and enjoy the Freak Show: my father's other cousin, Martika's uncle, had divorced recently and was now with a girlfriend who resembled the make-up mannequins in department stores. Martika's father and mother had already divorced, showing that twins can do more than just look alike. Her father said both wives had "gone alcoholic" on them: that's why they had custody of the kids, and why they were "on the prowl" again! Martika sneered at this phrase.

The mannequin had a truly weird son, about 8 years old, who was carrying around and shaking a box of breakfast cereal. His eyes were too small and too close together.

"He's just a cutie pie! Shore loves that cereal!" she said admiringly.

Suddenly he threw handfuls of the stuff into the air and said: "It's snowin' frosted flakes!"

Because a good amount of it landed in Martika's hair, she screamed an extremely low-class obscenity and her hand delivered a special package with extra postage to the side of the kid's head. This led to the mannequin screaming that nobody touches her child and suddenly the Freak Show was turning rather violent, with Martika's arms being restrained by her father and his brother holding back the swinging, swearing mannequin. The kid of course was squalling too, but then he decided to throw more of the cereal at Martika as she was being hauled off, which enraged her enough to break her father's grip and charge after the little cutie pie.

We left soon after that. On Sunday I told my parents I was going to visit one of my new friends from school. They of course just ate that up, because it meant that their plan to "socialize" me was working! So I hopped on my bike and took off for Sam's neighborhood.

I had not felt right in the last days about accusing Sam of lying: I thought if he has been lying, then I ought to feel justified. But in the end I really had no proof, just a suspicion that what he was telling me was phony and wasting my time. Poor detective work is based only on the right-side of the brain: too many emotions. That can get you hurt. I needed to do more Sherlock Holmes deducing from the facts.

One of the facts I wanted to uncover was the reason for Sam's disappearances from school. And I had a right-side-of-the-brain hunch that the reason was at his house. (Both sides of the brain have to work together!) So I thought scouting around where he lived would help me to answer why he missed school so much. I had to admit: this was not the rich side of town: it was more like the roach side. Boarded up houses here and there, even some burned-out houses. This neighborhood might make the pages of *Demolition Digest* but not much else.

I knew Sam was smart, but today I was about to be impressed by exactly how smart he was.

"What do you want here, on Sunday?" he asked me at the door.

"Why not? I already went to church. This seemed like the next best place."

"Why?"

"So I can tell you I'm sorry about pushing you, verbally, the last time we talked."

"It's true."

"What is?"

"What you said. It's all true."

You would think I wouldn't hate being right. But I did. So Sam did not just happen to be part of the group who discovered the body. He was just as terrified and traumatized as Anna, because somehow he saw at least something of the murderous act itself.

"Come on in," he said in a dull voice.

The house probably only had 5 rooms. The living room looked like a typical teenager's room. A video game system was attached to the T.V. set. A large stereo system dominated one end of the room. Some clothes-baskets were full of either dirty or clean clothes, and former pizza boxes were stacked up for some reason: maybe they could be used as insulation against the coming autumn and winter cold.

I walked into the hall and followed some odd smells with my nose. The kitchen had no curtains, no decorations, and the sink was full of dishes. Junk food residue was scattered over the counter, which was full of burn marks.

"Sam, tell me the truth now, since you're in the mood."
"The truth about what?"

"Do you have parents?"

"My dad's a truck driver. Long haul."

"How often is he home?" "Not very."

"Lucky guy! So you didn't have to be dragged off to church this morning."

"No, I went to church."

"You did? Of your own volition? Volition means..."

"Don't talk down to me! I know what volition means. And my volition wants you gone right now, if you don't change your attitude."

"Okay, okay. I just thought you might be sleeping in on Sunday instead of honoring the God of your choice."

"No, I always go to church every Sunday. It's the right thing to do."

"So you're a believer?"

"Yeah, I'm a believer."

I stood by a window and pointed outside to a bird in the backyard.

"What kind of Supreme Being would invent a world where robins have to eat worms?" I asked.

"At least the Supreme Being doesn't have you eating worms!" That much was true. Sam then turned to the sink and started the dish-washing ritual of waiting for hot water, rinsing off residue, and cleaning out the sink. I found a clean towel and offered to dry everything. For a long time Sam didn't say anything, and as I looked more and more at plastic dishes and cups with cartoon characters, another thought came to me.

"You have a little brother or sister?"

"You really are a detective."

I waved a cup from a fast-food joint with goofy-looking cartoon figures on it.

"You don't have to be much of a detective to deduce that this is probably not yours."

"Right. I've got a little brother. He's out visiting friends down the street."

I deduced right away that Sam was more than a big brother: he was also playing the father for his younger brother. This explained Sam's seriousness and could also explain the absences from school. It also placed Sam on a higher, more mature, more intelligent level than the others at school. This is why I wrote earlier that today I realized how smart Sam was. But another absence was not explained, and I decided not to ask: where was the mother?

There was silence while we finished and put everything away. Sam then went back to the living room and cleaned the dust from some things, then picked up the stack of pizza boxes and took them outside to a recycling tub.

"I usually keep things cleaner. It's just been hard to concentrate on stuff lately," he said.

"Maybe if you finally tell me what actually happened, you can give your mind some rest. Maybe things will make better sense."

Sam considered this for a few long moments. Then he nodded and began talking slowly:

"The lights were off. That's the first thing. It was dark and hard to see in the service area. I happened to be in early that day, 'cause I couldn't sleep."

"Which door did you use?"

"The one that leads to the loading dock."

This made sense so far, except for the part about a teenager not being able to sleep. Teenagers can always fall asleep, especially in our school. Anyway, the loading dock door was not visible from the inside door where Anna said she was standing, when she came to ask the janitor to open a rest room upstairs. So Sam and Anna could not have seen each other.

"And then?"

"I kept hearing some of these weird voices."

"How many weird voices?"

"I can't really say. Maybe just one. And that's why I thought the principal was involved."

"How's that?"

"This weird voice kept saying 'Kaplan' a couple times."
"You're sure about that?"

"Yeah, so that's why I thought later the principal did it."

"Then what happened?"

"Well, it was pretty dark down there, and I really couldn't see anything much, so I just called out 'Mr. Laurenz' twice, but nobody said anything at first. I heard some of these metal noises, but the place has all kinds of noises, you know, because of all the boilers and pipes and stuff. I didn't want to stumble around in the dark, so I went back out the door and walked around to the main entrance, went through the school, and then saw some of the other guys from the crew coming in. We went to our lockers first, then we walked down to the service area. And that's when...that's when we saw him hanging."

"What about the dark?"

"What? What about it?"

I had been thinking of what Anna said in her version. She also used the term "weird noises" just like Sam. That could be a coincidence, typical teenager talk. But Anna never said anything about the dark in the janitor's area.

"Why were the lights on? You said it was dark when you came in the other door. How did the lights get turned on?"

"I don't know."

"Did somebody on the crew turn them on?"

Sam looked thoughtful and stared off into space.

"I don't remember that. Maybe. But it seems like they were already on, when we got there."

"And you didn't see anybody else in the area?"

"You mean your other witness? This girl you know? No, nobody else was around. Or, I didn't see anybody at least."

This obviously meant that Anna had already recovered from her fainting spell and staggered off before the cleaning crew arrived. I was still wondering about the tight timing of all this: things sure worked out just perfectly for the murderer. The lights are out so the one possible witness can't see anything. And when the lights are on, the other witness faints and leaves in terror. The janitor's office and computer just happen to be available for writing that suicide note. Both witnesses have different stories, so even if you were the murderer and were caught somehow, even a D minus lawyer could shoot down these 2 stories. And then there's Aura Malper wrapped in plastic upstairs.

The official police story was looking better and better.

September 6

Early in the morning, at the same time Sam said he had walked through the loading dock door to the janitorial area, I did the same thing. It was time to re-create Sam's story. Everything was dark, and many mechanical noises hit my ears. I stood there for a few minutes and wondered how Sam might have focused on "metal noises" that morning. Still, if he was used to the usual noises, he probably could filter them out from the sounds of someone being strangled by a chain. I checked my watch and then left, retracing Sam's route to the main entrance. Here's where things became iffy. How much time did he spend with the crew and at his locker? I walked to his locker area and waited for a few minutes. Then I went back downstairs to the boiler room.

All of this took under 10 minutes, which I thought was a really tight time-frame. Plus, things were still fairly dark, although I could see more from this entrance, because of the glow from the hallway lights. I walked into the room and then the lights came on! I looked around to see if one of the other janitors had flipped a switch. Nobody was around! The only solution came to me: the lights were on a motion-sensor to save energy! I wondered why Sam had not known this, since he was on the work crew. But sometimes people just don't observe things: this probably meant nothing. I had to be careful about complicating everything. And yet...

Problem: why wouldn't all the motion of a murder trigger the lights to go on? I walked over to the pipe on the other side of the boilers where Dick Laurenz was found. A pair of pliers was lying there. I picked them up and put them in my pocket, then I checked my watch. Motion-sensor lights have timers, and after 3 minutes the lights went off. I waved my arms and walked around in a long ellipse and tried to trigger the lights again. Nothing. Solution: only if somebody walked in from the hallway would the sensor turn the lights on.

And Anna said she had walked into the area. The lights sensed her motion, and so that explained the contradiction. Just as I was thinking this, the lights in fact came on. I listened carefully and walked on tip-toe toward the boilers. Assuming that one of the janitors had walked in and triggered the lights, I listened and kept away from the office. The lights in the office flickered on, a chair creaked, and I heard the silly music of a computer firing up. Unlike Anna, I didn't faint, but just left.

"That's the narc!"

This sounded bad, and when I turned around it looked worse. My one deadhead Nazi and an evil-faced senior were coming at me fast. The deadhead Nazi was in the lead, so using my martial arts training, I grabbed the Nazi's shirt, fell backward placing my foot in the creep's stomach, and sent the bully screaming through the air to land with a crack and to hug the tile. The senior then tried to attack me, but I blocked two swings, and then pumped the air out of the kid's body with two kicks. The first kick put the body to its knees, the second brought the lips to the floor for a long cold kiss.

As they both gasped for air like dying fish on a beach, I remembered the pliers in my pocket. I quickly pulled them out and clamped them on the nose of the senior, who wanted to scream in pain, but the poor kid had no air left for a scream.

"Here's *my* little helper!" I said with a smile. "He doesn't breath, but he does have jaws. He just wants to give you a really tight squeeze, since he likes you so *much!*" and I applied just a little more pressure. "No, no, don't wiggle! That only makes the pain worse! Hold very, very still! Now here's what's going to happen! You and your posse will leave me and my friends alone, or Mr. Needle-Nose Pliers here will perform some facial surgery on you. You know, like getting rid of ugly things that stick out?"

Note how I have been able to avoid revealing if this was a girl- fight or a boy-fight, or maybe mixed! It doesn't matter actually. What did matter was another voice behind me.

"Hey! What happened here? Are they like...sick or something?"

I quickly hid my little helper. Annoying Lana was coming down the hall with a few others. The others mumbled a few words like "burn-outs" and "losers" without stopping to wonder why the two were hugging themselves. Lana looked at me in a different way. In fact, everything about her for a few minutes seemed more natural. She stood next to me with her hands on her hips in a "take-charge" stance. And her face had an expression of disgust and quick intelligence.

"This will complete your orientation tour of the school: meet the Ugly Bug Druggies, our resident deadhead Nazis," I said. "The big ugly bug is the main pusher and dealer, as far as I've heard. The little ugly one is a user-loser."

"And why're they on the floor?"

"Let's just say they had something Japanese for breakfast, like, you know, sushi and hand-chops, and it didn't agree with their stomachs."

Lana also wondered about the nosebleed on the ugliest one, but I suddenly forgot how that might have happened. We walked away quickly as the two were beginning to breathe normally again and tried to stand up.

"Is the one really a dealer?" asked Lana with hard eyes.

"Seems to be. It's what I've heard. I had a run-in earlier with the little scumbag, who was doing drugs in a bathroom," and I explained how Sam had helped me then, and how they had been sending him threats. I noticed that I was talking more to Lana now than I normally would, because she had lost the glowing dumbness that usually surrounded her.

"Doesn't the administration know?"

That was interesting. She used the word "administration" in that question. Yesterday's Lana would've said "the principal" or maybe "the teachers" in that question, not "administration" because it had 5 syllables. Lana was not a 5-syllable word girl. Or at least the Lana I knew before this updated version walked by today.

"They should, but haven't you seen Gorgeous George Kaplan? He wears bowties. Old guys with bowties ain't streetwise, y' know what I'm sayin' dudette?"

My mocking mean-streets tone took her by surprise.

"And *you* know all about it?" she said sarcastically.

"Not everything, but I've picked up on it enough around here Why? Are you a user?"

"Look at me!" and I stared at her. "Are you going to insult me again like that?"

I acted hurt, not threatening. "No, sorry, I should've known, but I just want to be sure."

"Now you're sure. Anyway, I've picked up on these things because I keep my eyes and ears open. You'd think everyone would be on red alert in a school that just had a murder-suicide."

"Yeah, you might think so. Where'd you learn the moves?" and she narrowed her eyes.

I told her the name of the martial arts school where I'd been training for most of the last 8 years. I'm not real big, but I'm not small either.

"Never had to use it until today. Sam and his broom intervened the last time, like I said. Looks like all the training was worth it."

"You aren't worried that they'll come back after you? You're that confident?"

Who was this Lana using a big word like "confident" correctly? Where were the 13 "likes" and "y' knows" in every stuttering thought?

"I can't worry about that. Spoils my fun here. Anyway, I know some people already: I think they'd come riding to the rescue. They'll watch my back, I hope!"

Clichés, but I was thinking and speaking at the same time. And what I was thinking involved Lana's personality. People, like, don't change like, y' know, change like, like this, like so totally, like overnight. But then slowly the usual Lana reappeared, especially when some girls came up to us.

"Say, like, what're you doing here so early anyway?" Lana asked me.

"I can ask you the same thing."

"Okay, so I was like thinking of joining the work crew in the morning. So, like, I thought I'd see the janitor and sign up."

Lana's new friends stood by us now: they were on the level of the previous Lana.

"Hey Lana! You really gonna, like, sign up for that work crew thingy?" asked the one, who dressed as if her phone number were 867-5309.

"If you do, maybe, like, maybe I will too."

I love peer pressure: if all your friends start cleaning toilets, does that mean you'll do it too? With these girls around the typical Lana returned. And that was the signal for me to leave.

And speaking of the work crew, I wondered where Sam was? Just late for work, or absent again for school? The halls were still pretty empty, so to be safe I went into the library. A lady librarian was now plopping down a book-bag and getting ready for a hard day of *not* checking out books and *not* looking anything up for anybody. It had to be the easiest job in the school. But she could at least act as a deterrent against a second assault by the drug bugs.

Among the five early birds in the library was Anna. She was doing homework. I sat down next to her.

"I have some information," I said. "It could help us in the case."

"What is it?"

"First I need you to remember something about that uniform."

"What?"

"I need you to remember the color."

She shook her head. "I don't know. It just happened too fast."

I didn't want to suggest any colors, so that her memory might not be affected by the suggestion.

"It's just that I have an idea on the kind of uniform you might've seen, but it depends on the color."

She shook her head again. "I don't know. I just want the whole thing to go away."

"Murders never go away. They're always there. Even when they're solved."

"I really don't like that kind of talk," she said.

"What kind?"

"The kind that wins arguments, even when it loses."

"Clever girl!"

I told Anna to meet me here after school, that I might have something for her. The other goal for the day was to track down Steve Cadosia, and the main way to track him down was to track down my new cousin Martika. I knew she had English first period, when I was supposed to be in World Geography. On Saturday she was complaining about having to read what she called a second-rate book: *A Separate Peace* by John Knowles. I objected to her opinion: that would be an insult to second-rate books. This fifth-rate book was a bad imitation of the classic over-rated adolescent loser book called *Catcher in the Rye,* whose author quite rightly went into hiding for most of his life after its publication. So after homeroom I spotted a boy carrying this book and asked him about Martika. Luckily they were in the same class, so I followed him to the room and waited.

"What do you want?" she asked without much interest.

"Some family picnic, huh?"

"Yeah, must've been a great show for the perfect side of the family. What do you want?"

"Not much. Tell me where I can find Steve Cadosia, or point him out, if he's around here."

Martika cursed rather loudly. "You lied to me! You're a narc!"

"Wrong twice."

"Right twice! You said there was nothing going on, and there obviously is, or else you wouldn't be asking about Steve."

"Look, I really don't know if anything is going on or not. I'm just passing the time, avoiding boredom, checking out some rumors."

"About Steve?"

"Not really, maybe only indirectly."

Martika spoke some unnatural curses against me for speaking indirectly.

"Hey, we're relatives!" I objected.

"Cousin of a cousin's not much of a relative," she said with a hateful tone.

"What's the matter with you?"

"You! Snooping around where you're not wanted! I don't know why you keep asking about Steve, but I'm warning you to stay away and keep your mouth shut. You don't know anything, you don't *understand* anything! You're just a little punk freshman, you're nothing, you're below nothing, you're less than worthless, so just get lost and stay lost!"

I have deleted all the very impolite and very low-class adjectives that she sprinkled in between some of her words. Martika was trapped in a gloomy creepy forest yet seemed to enjoy beating me with sticks from that forest. The bell was about ready to ring, so I left for World Geography.

Lana was motioning to me when I walked in. She wanted me to sit next to her. Since there were no assigned seats, I accepted her offer.

"Hey! You gotta be careful," she whispered.

"Why?"

"Y' know those 2 kids you beat up?"

"Wait: you mean the 2 kids who tried to beat *me* up!"

"Whatever! They're telling everybody you're a narc."

So that's where Martika got one of her insults.

"Yeah, well, so what?"

"So what? They're not the only ones, like, dealing and using drugs here, y' know? There are some kids here you really don't wanna mess with. If they think you're a narc, you can get hurt. I'm talkin' like hospital hurt."

"For a new kid, you've found out a lot in a short time. But don't worry. I can handle it."

Suddenly alarms went off in a special way. This was no fire drill. Everybody looked at each other, and then Mr. Raymond Dunwoody stood up from his desk and closed the door. He then told everyone to stay in the room and listen for an announcement. Within 30 seconds Mr. George Kaplan was broadcasting that there was a lockdown underway, that nobody was to leave the rooms where they were now sitting, and that any student found in the halls or restrooms would be "severely penalized."

Mr. Dunwoody tried to start class, but it was difficult for the kids to concentrate on identifying major cities of India. And right when he was explaining to a girl that South Dakota's Indian reservations had nothing to do with Calcutta, dogs began barking from down the hall.

"Drug dogs!" whispered several of the kids at once.

"Why're they here?"

"Must be a drug bust going down."

Bad timing! On the day that rumors are being spread that I'm a narc, on the day that I kebab 2 druggies, the police come to sweep the school for drugs! That will not seem like a coincidence! Mr. Dunwoody continued with the class, as if everyone were focused on his map of India. Some of the kids just could not stop whispering about who might be caught, and what they might be caught with. I listened to some of the lists of suspects and what they used or sold. Apparently there were students in our school whose lockers rivaled hospital pharmacies in selection.

And then guess what? Guess who gets marched by the windows of our classroom? My two attackers, Big Ugly Bug and Little Ugly

Slug, were being hustled down the hallway! That was good, but things were now looking less like a coincidence! What were the odds that the police would zero in on just these two, with all these other kids abusing drugs too? I wanted to know the evens as well as the odds on this.

Lana looked at me a few times during the class, but didn't whisper anything, although I thought she wanted to say something. When the bell rang, I headed off for Biology. Lana caught up with me in the hall.

"Hey, like I said, you gotta be careful today. Maybe all the time."

"Yeah, okay, but the main guys are off to juvie now, so I don't need to worry too much."

I began wondering more about Lana during Biology. Her personality changed, when she saw me slam-dunk the punks this morning. Why would something like that affect your speaking style? Why was she now so worried about my safety? She must be thinking of me as a friend. And yet we barely know each other! Maybe nobody else talks to her much, although she did have those two Twinkies with her this morning. They gave the impression of being a pod. And of course, there is a problem with this idea of Lana wanting to be my friend: I really don't like Lana much, as you already know. But if she changes her ways, maybe I'll like her better.

I looked for Martika during lunch. Something gnawed at me about her outburst this morning, and I wanted an answer.

But the only way to get it, I was somewhat afraid, was to reveal everything I knew. That would be premature. Anyway I found Martika at a table with a dark, very handsome boy. I thought about just idly walking by to see if I could get a nicer reaction, but they seemed to be a couple with an invisible shield around them. Staying away seemed wise for the moment.

Well, I thought, that explains things...maybe! Martika does not like me suddenly because my "snooping around" might lead to her parents discovering that she has a boyfriend. Maybe she is not allowed to have a boyfriend yet. Maybe that's what I "don't understand" at all!

During English at the end of the day I overheard two girls talking in the room about Aura Malper.

"It's been over a month now, y' know, since it all happened."

"Yeah, you're right. Things were kind of, I don't know, kind of creepy for a while, y' know?"

"Yeah, but now, things are kind of back to normal."

They were right. Memories were pretty well wiped clean in the last weeks, and you couldn't tell any longer that the school had suffered a trauma. The halls and cafeteria were noisy again. The school counselors had fewer visitors. Drug use obviously was up, and dirty graffiti appeared more and more in bathrooms and on the fence around the baseball field: yes, things were back to normal.

Dumblish class was reading *Fahrenheit 451* by Ray Bradbury. I already had gone through it a few years ago. Preachy science fiction is not my thing, but this book did allow Mr. Randolph to spend a week showing us the movie version. He had spent a week showing us the movie version of *The Old Man and the Sea*. Mr. Randolph was smart: every book he assigned had a movie version. In some cases he was also lucky: there were 2 movie versions of *The Hunchback of Notre Dame* by Victor Hugo, which was on the reading list for October. This book, I am positive, nobody in the class will read. The book has too many pages, and the pages have too many words, and the words have too many syllables. Three strikes and Victor Hugo walks back to the bench!

To build up the students' vocabulary, Mr. Randolph gave us lists of words that we were supposed to use in sentences. These sometimes gave me opportunities to avoid boredom. He called on me.

"Read us the sentence you wrote for the word 'fulsome' please." I read out proudly:

"Lincoln said: you can fulsome of the people some of the time." Among the smarter kids this caused a few snickers, but Mr. Randolph was in no mood to reward me with candy bars.

"You know better than that!" he scolded me in some disgust.

"I know many things better than that," I agreed.

"Puns are the lowest form of humor," he proclaimed the cliché proudly.

"Shakespeare used puns," I observed.

"You are not Shakespeare."

I had to agree. Mr. Randolph had good eyes and a good sense of time and place, even if his taste in books was not mine.

"You're right. I'm not Shakespeare. I can shake a stick, but I don't have a spear. But some kids shake their booty."

This caused some laughs, smiles, and groans. Eventually Mr. Randolph moved on: he gave me another chance to read a fulsome sentence without a pun. After class Mr. Clean and

Mr. Obscene, the two boys I had talked to once in the cafeteria, came up to me.

"Great way to waste time again!" said Mr. Clean.

"It's a gift," I said modestly.

"Hey! You still think that janitor was murdered?" asked Ollie Obscene.

"Yeah, maybe. Why?"

"We heard somebody saw it!"

"Who?"

"Don't know. It's goin' 'round that there was a witness."

This burned my ears. My rumor that I started with these two was that I had overheard the principal talking. It had nothing to do with a witness. But how many people were now involved in this? There was my erratic triangle: Emma knew about Anna, but not about Sam, and Sam knew about Anna, but Anna knew nothing about Sam.

On the fringe was Martika, who did not like my questions about Steve Cadosia and Aura Malper for some reason. But how did that translate into a rumor that a witness existed? And really on the fringe was Lana, who was also very curious in more ways than one. But Lana as the source for the rumor made no sense either.

"That witness ought to be careful," I said.

"Oh yeah? Why?"

"Because if there really is a murderer, I'd say any witness is next in line to be in a plastic garbage bag."

"Cool!" said Ollie Obscene.

"You really think there might be another murder?" asked Mr. Clean a little too eagerly.

"I hope not. But, can you two remember where you heard this rumor?"

"In the restroom. Some older guys were talkin' 'bout it."

The restroom! Source of all evil in the world! I nodded to them and headed to check the library to see if Anna was there yet. No Anna anywhere. I sat down and read a book for a few minutes: *The Invasion of Europe by the Barbarians* by J. B. Bury. The book has a relevance that is unsettling as one looks around a school hallway and cafeteria. It is also relevant to an unread library devoid of students. Finally Anna walked in and saw me.

"So what is this 'something' you were talking about?" she asked as she frowned at the title of the book.

"Steve Cadosia. Does that name mean anything to you?"

"Is he on the football team maybe?"

"I don't know. But his name has come up. He's an ex-boyfriend of Aura Malper's. It's the first lead I have on Aura's murder."

"A lead to what?"

"I don't know: only guesses and possibilities. But..." and I whispered now, "ex-boyfriends have been known to become violent." Anna nodded seriously with wide eyes, and then slumped in the chair and stared into nowhere. Finally she said:

"I'm tired. I can't take all this pressure," and she began to confess to me that she had started trying to escape everything. "I know it's stupid, but my mom has some old pills that she got from a doctor to help her sleep, when she was stressed. I've been taking some of those, just to help me sleep at night, you know, all the way through. They work, but then I feel like I can't get going. So I've been drinking lots of caffeine with a cold pill now and then, just to get going."

"You know this is bad for your body and brain in all kinds of ways," I said in a neutral tone."

"I know, and I'm gonna stop, as soon as I can get over this. It's just, it's just everything is still in my head. But I'll stop, I'll stop, it'll be okay."

"You should tell your parents, at least your mom. She'll want to know what's been happening."

"No, 'cause if I tell her I've been stealing her pills, she'll want to know why, and then I'd have to tell her that I was there, when Mr. Laurenz was killed, and then she'll want me to go to the police!"

"Which is what I've been telling you too."

"No, I don't know, no, I just want all this to go away," and her face headed toward her lap. Anna started crying and shaking.

"Have you noticed that the pills don't make it go away?" I commented quietly.

"Yeah, you're perfect. You know everything," and she wiped her face. This was not my day to deal with people playing too tight violin strings! Anna now was becoming hostile, just like Martika.

"They say the first step to solving a problem like yours is to admit that the problem exists. You've done that now with me. Take the next step. You've confessed to me, now confess to your parents."

Anna stared at a set of encyclopedias. Then she closed her eyes and sighed.

"I guess you're right. But I can't do it. Not yet."

September 7

The school was full of chatter today about the drug bust, and as a result I was getting nods and sneers from some kids in my classes. No doubt now: to some of them I was an official police spy, responsible for ratting out Big Ugly Bug and Little Ugly Slug. And how many others would be marched out to police cars in the next days? And how many of them would actually be innocent, falsely accused by the narc? And how much did the narc get paid? Did they pay the narc per accusation?

Fortunately it's a big school, and I can keep a low profile. Lana was not in school today, so nobody was whispering to me in first period. To avoid any possible trouble in the cafeteria I decided to hide out in the library during lunch: I also had an idea. Yearbooks would have a picture of Steve Cadosia! I would at least be able to recognize him, if I came across him somewhere. The library had a complete collection of school yearbooks going back decades.

But on the way I passed by Einsteinland, also known as the Physics lab, and saw Emma Risley as I glanced in. I was impressed: how many science classes did she take? She was fiddling around with some wires, but her music wasn't pretty.

"You really shouldn't talk like that," I said with a smile.

"Unless you're here to tell me that dumb cow has gone to the police, get out!"

"I'm here to tell you that I need some information about a guy called Steve Cadosia. And I'm also here to tell you that you're connecting that circuit the wrong way."

"So now the kid detective's a big Physics expert!" and Emma's face steamed out frustration and threw down the needle-nose pliers. I picked them up along with a screwdriver and switched two wires. I then twirled the pliers and said:

"Second time this week I've used pliers like this!"

"What's that mean?"

"Private joke. So what can you tell me about Steve Cadosia?"

"He's on the football team. Big guy. That's about all I know. Is he connected to the case?"

"I'm still wondering about Aura Malper. He was her boyfriend some months ago."

"And so what's the connection? You think he killed her?" and Emma's tone was very skeptical about that.

"I really have no evidence, except that ex-boyfriends are known to become violent."

"But why would he have killed my uncle?"

"That's what I don't know. Maybe your uncle saw him strangling Aura, or at least saw him with the body afterwards, when he was stuffing her into the garbage bag. He chases him downstairs, where your uncle is trying to get to a phone. He strangles him, types the suicide note on his computer, and that's when Anna appears at the door, and faints when she sees your uncle hanging from that pipe."

Emma thought about that for a few moments. Then she said:

"I don't know. That's an awful lot of smart thinking for a football player in a short time."

"Don't give into the cliché that all football players are dumb. They can do quite a bit of fast thinking under pressure on the field."

"That's different," said Emma. "That's just quick reflexes. We're talking about some real thinking, about how to frame my uncle for a murder, in just a few minutes. And doing it after killing Aura. That's one cold, hard killer."

Emma was right, and everything she said is what bothered me from the beginning about any alternative explanation. Still, even though he might be a football player, Steve Cadosia could be smart enough and cool enough to pull something like this off.

Suddenly, as I thought again about the timing of everything, a new interpretation came to me. Emma went back to her circuit board.

"Backwards!" I said.

"Not any more it isn't," she said, thinking I meant her circuit board.

"No, the murders could be backwards!"

Emma frowned, looked at me carefully, and asked: "What're you talking about?"

"We've been following the police in all of this, except that we've been looking for a third person. The police explanation has your uncle killing Aura first, and then committing suicide in despair. But if there's a third person, a person who has planned things out, they might've killed your uncle first, and then Aura. The order of the murders might actually be backwards."

"Okay, but why?"

"Why is the question that has no answer yet, except for the police answer."

"The police answer has to be wrong: no suicide, no stalking, no obsession. Not by my uncle," and Emma was becoming angry again. "If this Steve Cadosia's involved, then I ought to look into this myself," and she was gritting her teeth. "A month's gone by, and you should see my mom, still depressed, crying, going to a psychiatrist for therapy and pills that don't work. My dad's become invisible, comes in late, falls asleep on the couch so he doesn't have to deal with my mom."

"I'm sorry," I said. "I wish I were older, a real detective: maybe I'd have everything solved by now."

"Don't be stupid: you've got no reason to be sorry. None of this is your business."

"I feel like it is, because of Anna. She's pretty messed up too: she confessed something to me that, well, means she's messed up."

"If she went to the police, they'd re-open the case, and she wouldn't be feeling guilty and wouldn't be messed up! I don't have any sympathy for her."

"Tell me something I don't know."

"Here's something you don't know: you want a confession? I'll give you one: if I find the murderer first, he's dead."

I just smiled and nodded in disbelief. "You think I don't mean it?"

"That's right: I think you don't mean it." "Then you think wrong."

"You think you'd really be able to kill somebody?"

"Not just somebody: the somebody who killed and framed my uncle. I'd have no problem taking him out permanently."

"And you think that'd solve all your family's problems? Everything goes back to the way it was?" I asked in disbelief.

"No, but it would make me feel a whole lot better! And I'd do it slowly too, just to make sure the killer paid full price. No discount K-Mart executions."

Emma was confessing a little too openly, a little too easily, about her executioner's fantasy. I still believed she didn't mean any of it, although my memory did bring up that day in the Biology lab, where she was slicing and dicing that fetal pig. But there was really no way a girl as smart as Emma Risley could actually execute anybody, even the murderer of her uncle.

"Okay," I said, playing along. "Revenge for the family honor: I can see that you're actually kind of old-fashioned, Emma."

"Yeah, that's right. 'Revenge for the family honor': I like the way that sounds." She paused. "So, what if the murders are reversed? How does that help us? Where's it lead?"

"That's what I'm not sure about. That's why I want to talk to this Steve Cadosia. I was just on the way to the library to check out his picture in a yearbook."

"Good idea," she said, and then added: "You're pretty smart, even if you are just a freshman."

So I sauntered into the library, which was fairly deserted as always. The yearbooks were kept against a back wall. Because they cost a lot of money, and because the Yearbook Class makes sure the pictures are mostly of themselves and their friends, not too many people buy a yearbook. So the library has 2 or 3 copies for every year, which they chain to the wall because, like I just said, the books are expensive. Of course the chains don't stop some kids from stealing a yearbook. The chains are seen as a challenge to their criminal ingenuity. Two little brackets hold the chains onto the wall, and the brackets are held by two screws. With a small screwdriver and a minute of time you can have a free yearbook!

Fortunately last year's copies were still around. They had been defaced and otherwise vandalized here and there with inky mustaches and obscene comments and pictures. I opened the mug shot section to last year's sophomores and carefully scanned the pictures. My finger moved quickly through the B names and slowed down when I hit C. Steve Cadosia should be near the beginning of C. There he was, and I tapped my finger on the name, and then my eyes focused carefully on the small photograph of a dark, handsome boy.

Probably I looked pale as I realized who Steve Cadosia was. I had already seen him! And I will admit that my legs and arms trembled just a little now. Several plausible possibilities linking Steve Cadosia to the murders circled and hovered in my mind. In one version he murders Aura in a fit of rage upstairs, but is caught by the janitor as he disposes of her body in the garbage bag. He chases the older man down, and murders him outside the janitor's office, where Anna then appeared at the wrong time. And on that day Steve just happened to be wearing that JROTC uniform.

In a second scenario Steve has an accomplice, who greatly simplifies the completion of a double murder. In this scenario the two of them are murdering Aura Malper, and then one runs off to kill Mr. Laurenz, after he sees what they've done. It doesn't much matter who kills whom. The accomplice was...is...big enough to have killed Mr. Laurenz. In a third scenario, Steve and his accomplice plot to frame Mr. Laurenz with Aura's murder, which also solves the difficulty with timing. This third version is the one that seemed to fit best, even if it was the most horrible version, because everything was so premeditated. It would allow the murders to be reversed, like I had thought, or maybe allow them to happen simultaneously.

And so why would Steve Cadosia kill his old girlfriend? Jealousy, anger, and the old stories: maybe his new girlfriend wanted him to prove his love. Maybe his new girlfriend was the violent, jealous one. She wore a uniform too: I had seen it in her closet.

The closet of his new girlfriend, my cousin, Martika.

September 9

Yesterday I played sick. My mother would have thought it was early in the year to have a cold, so I contracted mysterious stomach pains. The cause could be anything: without a fever there would be no doctors. I just was a victim of that famous disease known as "one of those 24-hour bugs going around."

All day long I played Bach's famous composition *The Well-Tempered Clavier*: 24 keyboard pieces in 24 different keys. Sure: you probably have no idea what I'm talking about. Who was Bach? What's a clavier? What kind of nerd listens to that boring crap? What kind of pathetic out-of-it loser am I? All I can say is: I like it, and it helps me think.

Bach had 24 keys, but all I needed was one. Instead I had 3 keys to the murders, which I kept rotating while lying in my bed. Actually, it seemed more and more like one key with 3 sides. The result was always the same: the door opened to the deaths of two people. And I remembered Martika staring into space, talking about pain and emptiness and death. Aura's death seemed to upset her. Did that come from the remorse of the killer? Or was it survivor's guilt, like she said? Feeling bad because you're actually happy that you're the one who's alive and not the girl who's dead? Or feeling bad because you're the one who killed her?

As Bach continued with his exploration of B minor, I came back to something that had troubled me from the beginning. My scenarios were more complicated than the police explanation: I still wanted simplification. Things just did not seem right in my versions. By adding a killer, or killers, I was adding complication, and that did not seem to be the right path to solving the crime.

And trust me: I really did not want to add Martika or her boyfriend Steve as killers. I will confess that I was torn between not wanting her to be involved, and a feeling that my theory was too true. I kept going over everything, beginning with Anna's story. Everything hinged on it: if she doesn't see that figure, wearing a kind of uniform, holding onto the chain, if she doesn't hear that voice in her ear, then the whole

thing is false. Then there's Sam, who doesn't see anything, but thinks he hears "weird noises" and somebody saying the principal's name, Kaplan, maybe more than once, while the murder is taking place. Both of those details crash the police version.

So I kept coming back to Martika, and her JROTC uniform, and Steve Cadosia, who also had a JROTC uniform, and their reason for killing Aura and Mr. Laurenz. Love, teenagers in love, teenagers who think they know everything about love: the news had stories every week about how stupid teenagers can be, and dangerous, when they think they're in love, and have everything in life figured out. Okay, so I'm a teenager too, but you already know that I'm not typical. I'll confess I don't know everything about love and life, or life and love. Or hate and death, as far as that goes. But things worked out in my imagination only if Martika and Steve Cadosia, stupid and dangerous and in love, worked together to kill Aura and Mr. Laurenz.

Bach's great work came to an end after lunchtime. My mother had driven downtown to do some shopping. I dozed off watching an old detective movie on cable. I thought maybe it would help me, but I figured everything out before the Second Act. The telephone woke me up.

"So, you're home today?" asked a girl's voice.

"Martika?"

"Yeah, it's me, and guess what you missed at school today!"

"Hard to say. Mr. Kaplan get arrested?"

"Kaplan? Why would he get arrested?"

"Oh, I don't know. Dealing drugs? Murder maybe?"

"I'm not sure if you're trying to be funny, but if you are, you're not funny."

That was an interesting comment: especially the way Martika said it. She sounded insulted that I would say that Kaplan was a drug dealer or murder suspect.

"Why isn't that funny?"

"Sure, act stupid. Be that way. I should've known! You know all about everything that happened today. That's why you can make stupid jokes like that. Narc!"

"I really don't know what happened today, and I'm not so important that the police would want me to be an undercover teenage cop to find the druggies at school."

"That's really hard to believe."

"And anyway, what if I really were a narc? Why would that be bad? Why would getting rid of the jerks who sell drugs be a bad thing?"

"Didn't you pay attention in kindergarten? Nobody likes a tattle- tale!"

"Actually I never went to kindergarten."

"Yeah, always smarter than everybody else, ain'tcha?"

"Actually, no. But thanks for the compliment. Anyway, so what happened? I really don't know what you're talking about."

She hung up, after cursing me with words not found in any dictionary. She still believed I was working for the police. Problem: why was Martika so hostile to me because of this narc-business? Solution: she was a druggie. Or maybe her boyfriend Steve Cadosia was, or they both were. Those were the only explanations. I recalled her outburst earlier: "You don't understand anything." What didn't I understand? If Steve Cadosia sells or buys drugs, what's left to understand? On the other hand, another explanation existed: maybe she really just doesn't like "tattle-tales" at all. Maybe her parents don't know that Steve and Martika are "friends." Maybe they're against her having a boyfriend.

Maybe, maybe, maybe! I couldn't leave the house, since I was supposed to be sick. But I had to find out what Martika was talking about. There was no answer at Anna's house, so I called Sam. He sounded nervous.

"You gotta tell me the truth!" he said. "Always. What's going on?"

"Are you working for the police?"

"No."

"Why weren't you at school today?"

"I'm pretending to be sick. And that's the truth. So what was this big happening?"

"There was an assembly, and Mr. Kaplan told us that there had been an undercover cop working in the school to find out who was buying and selling drugs."

"Oh great! I picked a fine day to skip school! And so everybody thinks I'm the undercover cop now?"

"I don't know about everybody, but, you know, after everything that's happened with those kids and you, I thought maybe, you know, maybe it could've been you."

"No, trust me, that's just been a coincidence. And try not to say 'maybe' right now."

"Why?"

"Inside joke. So what else happened?"

"Not much: he said he was happy that the school didn't seem to have a big drug problem. The kids who were caught were probably the main ones involved, maybe, whoops, sorry, uh, he said they *might* be the *only* ones involved."

"There's a fantasy for you."

"Yeah, well, anyway, he said the undercover cop is gone now, but that just set people off wondering if it was a trick, you know, to get the other druggies to get careless. Maybe, uh, sorry, the cop could still be around."

"So either way, the kids are going to think I'm the narc. I shouldn't've skipped today."

"Why did you?"

"I wanted to think about the case. And because I'm actually stupid, I thought taking the day off might calm down all those 'narc' rumors about me."

"So, what about the case?"

"I've got a couple new theories, but no evidence about anything. I don't know. Maybe the police have it right after all."

"You said 'maybe'."

"I know. Like I said: just an inside joke."

A thought came to me. "Are you working tomorrow morning?" I asked.

"Yeah. Why?"

"I need to see the other crime scene. That cleaning supply closet upstairs."

"It'll be locked."

"But it has to be open sometime."

"They clean the upstairs after school. It might be open then."

"Why 'might be open'? Won't it be open for sure, if they're cleaning?"

"Well, no, you remember, 'cause they had it taped off right after the murder, and then, it kind of creeped everybody out, so the upstairs crew just carried stuff up from downstairs."

Of course I remembered: right after the murders kids were putting flowers and stuffed animals in front of the closet door. Then the school moved the memorial for Aura to a corner of the main hall. Too many toys and flower pots were blocking the hallway.

"Still, I need to see it," I said.

"But why?"

"I've seen the other crime scene, the janitor's area. To be complete, I should see where they found Aura's body."

"What do you think you'll find that the police didn't?"

"No idea, it's just that, if I'm going to investigate this thing the right way, I need to see it. So, if it's locked, can you get a key for it?"

"Well, maybe. I don't know. There's a board with keys on it inside the janitor's office. That's where the key probably is."

"So, can you see if you can get it?"

"I'll see what I can do."

There was some noise in the background, and then I heard Sam talking to somebody.

"Sorry," he said.

"Is that your father?" I asked.

"Uh, no. My little brother."

"Where is your father?"

"He's still on the road."

I had to wonder how often this father really showed up at home.

And again I wondered to myself about Sam's mother. But I didn't press him for an answer right now.

So today in First Period I showed up for World Geography, and there was Lana, standing by the door as if she were waiting for somebody. And she was waiting for somebody: me.

"Hey, like, where were you yesterday?"

"Home," I said cautiously.

"So you heard about everything, I guess?"

"Yeah, I heard about everything."

"So, like, you don't think you're gonna have anything to worry about?"

"I guess I'll find out today."

"You want me, like, to hang around with you today, just in case somebody tries something?"

So now you are wondering whether I will reveal if I'm a boy or a girl. If I'm a boy, it would be a great thrill to have an almost 17- year old girl "to hang around" me. Everyone would wonder what the attraction was between us. If I'm a girl, it would still be a thrill "to hang around" one of the older girls. Freshmen girls would hardly be in the same league as girls from junior year. But whether I'm a boy or a girl, the answer to Lana was still the same.

"No, thanks, I can take care of myself."

We walked into the classroom and sat down. If anybody in this class thought I was an informer for the police, they didn't show it. Of course few kids in this class showed much of anything, including consciousness. Mr. Raymond Dunwoody seemed happy to see me: it meant somebody would be answering his World Geography questions, which a retarded cow could answer really. I glanced around the classroom as the minutes dripped by, and nobody seemed to care about my presence.

But double-period Biology was different. During the lab two kids walked by me and whispered: "Fink!" This was an ancient insult, maybe designed to confuse me. I also heard "Rat!" as well as the usual "Narc!" When one kid sneered at me about helping the police, I just hissed:

"Sounds like you're nervous about something, friend."

"You're the one that better be nervous, friend."

"You got something to say? Come out and say it."

"Oh, I'm scared now."

"You will be," I whispered. "You will be!"

Bullies have never bothered me, as you already know. Part of that was due to my martial arts training, and another part just came naturally. Like I've said, I'm not real big, but I'm not real small either. There were limits, of course, to how many punks I could handle: but the last time, with the aid of my little needle-nosed friend, was no problem.

Now it was lunchtime, and to avoid more confrontations, I went to the library. Anna was there.

"So, have you told your parents about your problem?" I asked.

"It's been hard," she said, looking at the floor.

"You mean, it's been hard keeping your secret away from them."

"You always know everything. You always know everything better."

"No, not everything. But we're talking about your problem, and your parents have to know that you're medicating yourself."

"I'm not."

"You mean you're not on anything today. I can tell you're depressed, or that your brain isn't sure any longer what it wants. Should I take some uppers, or some downers, or just stay clean for a day, and then maybe just half a dose tomorrow? Maybe just one of the little speckled capsules, or maybe just pop half a Christmas tree. And then I can quit."

"There you go again: you know everything that's in everybody's head," and she seemed about ready to cry.

"Look," I said as softly and gently as I could, "I know that voice is still in your head. And I know you're scared. But you've got to stay clear-headed. You can't do this because...."

There was a long pause as my own thoughts suddenly entered new territory.

"Because why?" she asked.

"Because it's unhealthy."

But that wasn't what I was thinking. Martika and Steve Cadosia came into the library. If they were the murderers, if one of their voices had whispered into Anna's ear, then right now everything was over. Anna and I together would obviously lead them to one conclusion, and it wouldn't be pretty.

"Hey Steve!" said Martika. "There's my cousin, the undercover cop! Rat anybody out today, cuz?"

"Your assumptions are all wrong, Martika."

"I don't think so."

"Look: I'll ask it again. If I am helping the police catch drug dealers, which I'm not, how is that bad?"

"And I'll say it again: nobody likes a snitch, especially ones who go out of their way to snitch."

Steve Cadosia seemed not to understand what we were saying.

When he looked at Martika, his face showed the loyal adoration of a puppy saved from a life in the rain and from canine cuisine stuck in garbage cans. Ignoring Martika, I looked at him and said:

"So you're Steve. Glad to meet you at last." He looked confused and said:

"Why? You been lookin' for me or somethin'?"

"I just wanted to say how sorry I am about Aura. I heard you were her friend."

"That's enough!" said Martika nastily, adding a few nasty expressions to her new nastiness. "We never know if the snitch is looking to frame somebody and ruin their lives."

"Name one person I've ruined," I said.

"How about those kids they arrested?"

"Not because of me: the drug dogs caught them. But who cares if druggies are scratching out tic-tac-toe games on jail walls? Serves them right, don't you think, Steve?"

He glanced at Martika and seemed to hope she would give him a clue to the right answer.

"Well, yeah, but snitching for the cops ain't right either," he said finally.

"That's where you're wrong," I shrugged. "Anyway, I'm not working for the cops."

"Yeah, well, how about her? Or some of your other little friends?" and Martika pointed at Anna.

I decided it was time to reveal what was happening, and why I was "snooping around" to use Martika's words. This was a risk, of course, if they were the real murderers, but after seeing Steve in person now, I no longer believed he could be involved in killing anyone. With Anna's approval I gave a whispered summary of her entire role, including the killer's threat, and also including Sam's role, but I didn't use his name. As I said all of this, I carefully watched their faces, just to be sure of where they stood. They became more and more amazed, and Martika softened slightly.

"So the cops don't know about you?" Martika asked Anna.

"No, I just can't do it," and she gulped. "I get half sick just thinking of what would happen. The only times when I feel better are when I think I just imagined that voice."

That was an interesting comment: if Anna hallucinated everything out of shock, then the police version comes back. Sam's story could be explained away as simply mishearing something. Maybe the janitor was mumbling the name "Kaplan" as he typed his suicide note on the computer. There's that simple solution again!

Martika motioned that we should sit down at a table. Steve Cadosia pulled a chair out for her first. He looked extremely troubled.

"I hate to say it, but if there is a murderer, and he saw her by the door, why didn't he just kill her then and there?"

"Yeah," said Martika, "if you just killed two people, what's another one?"

"Time," I said. "He was running out of time. The school was filling up, and maybe he thought it would be too risky."

Nobody said anything for a few long seconds.

"So this is what all your questions and snooping around have been about?" asked Martika. I nodded. She looked over at Steve.

"Okay. So what did you want to know from Steve?"

"Well, did the police talk to you about anything, when they were here investigating? Anything about Aura?"

"No."

"And did Aura ever say anything about Mr. Laurenz?"

"No, why would she?"

"That's just the thing about the official story," I said. "Stalkers usually have some sort of contact with the people they're after. Notes shoved into a locker, or 'accidental meetings' that aren't accidental, or at least smiles or something like that."

"She didn't say anything to me, but..." and he became silent.

"But what?"

"After we broke up, well, you know, we didn't talk much. We were still friends and all that, but, you know. Just not the same way as before."

"Why'd you break up?"

"She said she needed more time to work on her grades, college and scholarships and stuff. I thought we had enough time to be a couple, but she didn't."

Martika looked at me carefully and said:

"So you guys going to the police with this story?"

"That's up to Anna, and she says she's not ready."

Anna sighed and said: "What would I tell them now? I sometimes don't know what I really remember and what I don't want to remember. Everything gets kind of fuzzy and all mixed up. It's been so long ago."

The bell rang, and I felt that everything was going cold. Everything hinged on Anna, and only a little bit on Sam. Emma had only the family loyalty to back up her belief that somebody else had to be the killer. But now I wanted to clear something else up.

"So, Martika, are we okay with each other now?" I asked.

"Yeah, I guess so. I just really don't like snitches."

Martika must have had a drama-trauma in kindergarten with a tattle-tale!

We went off to our classes. In the last period, Theoretical English, I would see Anna again. Mr. Randolph tried to have a discussion about the short story by O. Henry called *The Ransom of Red Chief*. This was difficult to do when practically nobody had the read the story. He was positive, because he was an optimist, that everyone *would* read the story, because it was a *short* story, and it was rather funny! But the aliens had already replaced most of the kids' brains with spores: they could only tune in to electric stuff. A short story, or a long story: where's the plug? Where's the on-off button? So I and two others talked with him about the story. Anna was not among them: she was zoned out.

The day was over at last. I wanted to go upstairs to the closet where Aura's body was found.

"Why don't you come with me?" I asked Anna.

"No, I've had it with this. I just want it to go away. I'm sorry I ever said anything to you about any of it. I think, I think it really maybe never did happen."

"Where's this change of heart coming from?"

"I'm tired and scared. And I'm tired of being tired and scared."

"That could be the pills talking. Did you stop taking them yet?" Anna looked down at the floor: "Sort of."

"Look: this is important. Did you hear that voice or not? Did you see another person or not? If you did, then let's go to the police and see what they say."

"No, I just want it all to go away. It was just a dream from when I fainted, because I saw Mr. Laurenz hanging there. That's all it was," and she started crying.

This attracted one of the janitors, an official janitor, not one of the students. He glanced at us and seemed to wonder why Anna was crying: we were standing by the steps, and he was on his way upstairs. Again he slowly observed us up and down, but then turned on the landing and disappeared from sight. This was a great opportunity to peek into the upstairs closet. He would probably go right to it.

"Are you with me or not?" I asked Anna. "We can follow him and take a look at the other crime scene."

Anna sighed, and then decided to go along.

Sure enough, the janitor was jangling his keys and headed for the closet where Aura's body had been found in the black plastic garbage bag. We walked halfway down the hall, then stopped. I acted like I was opening a locker, and then I dropped my schoolbag and rooted through it.

"Where is he?" I asked Anna.

"He's still in the closet. No, he's coming out now with a big dust mop."

"Tell me when he goes into a classroom."

"It's okay. He just walked into one."

I hurried over to the closet, and for some reason the swishing of my clothes seemed very, very loud. The door was half open, and a single light-bulb was on. I saw the usual things you would expect: bottles of toilet cleaner, mops, rags, rolls of the large black plastic garbage bags, and so on. But then as my eyes focused in the grayness, I was shocked and startled by something.

I backed out of the closet, and just then the janitor came out of the classroom he was dusting. He glared at me, and then focused on Anna down by the locker.

"What's goin' on? Tryin' to steal somethin'?" he said in a threatening tone.

"No, just walking by, and just, you know, happened to look inside."

"You ain't got no right t' be lookin' inside at nothin', so just keep on walkin'."

The janitor was wearing gloves. Heavy gloves. He was fairly big, with greasy hair and sideburns, the long kind that some losers think are always in style. There were some large moles on his face, and his teeth were too yellow for his age, which was probably 30 or so. And then the most obvious thing about him sent a shock through my legs and arms. I might even have gasped, but I think I caught it and instead I felt my face redden.

He wore a uniform with the name "Al" embroidered on a pocket flap. He wore a uniform!

He wore a uniform! And he had just used a triple negative: *You **ain't** got **no** right t' be lookin' inside at **nothin'**!* What was one of those whispered lines in Anna's ear? "Don't tell nobody nothin'!"

And inside the closet there was a chute, to send trash bags directly down to the dumpster.

And as I backed away and tried to act normal, everything came together in a flash. I should have known! Sometimes the choice between 2 answers is that they are both right! The police were right, but so were we! A janitor had killed Aura Malper and wrapped her body in plastic: this janitor, right in front of me, looking more and more suspicious.

I was looking at the killer!

This janitor, with gloves on, wearing a uniform, was the one stalking Aura! And when he strangled her that morning, and was about to dump her body down the chute, something goes wrong. He gets interrupted, maybe by Mr. Laurenz: there's a chase to the basement, where he kills Mr. Laurenz. Or maybe he strangles Mr. Laurenz here, puts his body in one of the bags, and decides to frame him for Aura's murder by faking the suicide.

No. Too complicated.

Simpler: it was all premeditated. He wanted Aura's body found. He wanted Dick Laurenz framed. He had planned everything. Killing for thrills, killing to show how smart you were, killing for fun, killing to prove you could fool all the police and all these teachers with their college degrees, when you were "just" a school janitor! That's why he never dumped Aura's body down the chute. Nothing had gone wrong and nobody had seen them here. He wanted her body found here! If it had been weird love gone violent, he would have sent that bag with her body down the chute. She gets buried in the city dump. And so the news tells about another teenager running away from home and disappearing. Yawn time.

But that would not be good enough for this guy: he wanted the thrill, the roller-coaster ride of walking around the school and watching the detectives put their explanation together. Problem: it's an explanation that he's made for them, and they swallow it, like birds eating a trail of bread crumbs and hopping into a trap. But now he's on top of the world! The Perfect Crime! By Al the Janitor.

Except it wasn't perfect. There was Anna, in a faint. How much did she see? How much did she hear? How much would she remember? A third murder wasn't part of the plan, and there were voices around. What to do? Under pressure he might make a mistake if he killed Anna. So he whispers that threat. And maybe he hopes that if she does talk to the police, they'll just think it's a part of the shock of seeing whatever she saw.

So in a way, the crime is still perfect. Everything is still working for him. I tried to act cool and slowly sauntered back to Anna.

"Is he still watching us?" I asked.

"Yeah. Did he get mad or something?"

"Maybe. Not really."

"What's wrong?" she asked with a frown.

I had a choice to make: I could tell her that I just solved the case, which was worthless because I had no proof at all. I could tell her that Janitor Al back there was the murderer who whispered the threat while she was on the floor. Maybe that would spook her enough to go to the police finally. Then we would know whether they would take her seriously or not.

Suddenly Lana appeared with one of her 5-watt friends. They had buckets and cleaning supplies.

"Oh wow, it's you again!" she said. "Like, have you seen Uncle Al up here? We just finished the girls' restroom and he needs to, like, you know, check it out, and then we can go."

"Yeah, I said, he's up here. Down the hall by that closet. But does he know you call him Uncle Al? He doesn't seem too friendly to me."

"Oh yeah, he's really cool, y' know?" said Miss Dimbulb.

"That guy? Cool? No way!" said Anna. "I don't like the way he looks."

"Oh nooo," droned Lana. "You don't know 'im. He's, like, a really nice guy."

We left, and I didn't feel good about any of this. Was Lana truly, deeply so dull to think that Uncle Al was "really nice" somehow? Like they say in fourth-rate movies: I had a bad feeling about all of this.

"I think you need to tell your story to the police," I said to Anna. "No, I'll never be able to."

"Well, if you don't tell them, then I will. Today. Right now." "No! You can't!"

"We've got to get this out in the open."

Anna sighed and then said: "Let me think about it one more day."

"Without mommy's pills? Or daddy's? You need to think straight about this."

"I promise. Just give me one more day."

September 10

Today I'm playing sick again. A relapse. I've been going back to Bach to clear my thinking. I wanted proof for my solution to crack the perfect crime. The only proof, a very tiny proof, was Anna, who could identify nobody. There really is no proof in this proceeding, your honor. My client is innocent. Case dismissed. If I go to the police alone, what will they think? A freshman playing detective! What a riot! Get outta here kid and go back to recess.

It's noon. I'm bored. I should've gone to school. No ideas on what to do, except to call Anna later and see what she has decided. It's 4 o'clock, and Anna isn't home yet.

It's 7 o'clock, and there's no answer at Anna's house.

It's 11 o'clock, and the news said Anna was found dead in our school's bathroom around 6:00 P.M. The police suspect either suicide or an accidental drug overdose. Bottles of pills were found in her possession.

Another case closed.

Conclusion

Honestly, we're pretty sure the case is NOT closed. It was grueling going through the handwritten pages of these journals. There were many scribbled marks, none of which we could make sense of. We couldn't think of a way to convey the feeling of the oil and grease marks, for instance, on page 34 of journal two or what we're sure is a small blood smear on page 78. This writing has a texture and depth to it that just doesn't translate well to the typewritten page. It's almost as if the pages are alive. But then again, we don't want to make too much out of what could just be curious, unrelated circumstances. Maybe the bloodstains came from a paper cut and just got smeared innocently across the page. And maybe we shouldn't read any symbolism into the noose-like shape the oil stain made. Sometimes, an oil mark is just an oil mark and means nothing more than that.

So we are off onto our next journey: one of us will cull through the journals and type as we read, almost in a state of somnambulism where hours slip away. At some point, you get so immersed in the material that you feel affection towards it – and you're typing, it seems, as fast as you're reading. You're anticipating the next word, then the next phrase, sentence, moment, and before you know it, you've typed in an entire chapter. There is a point where you disappear into a trancelike state and everything is seen through the narrator's eyes; you become the storyteller to someone else's nightmare: indeed, it's more than a little creepy – it's dangerously addictive! Thank God we have each other – to spot check what we've transposed for accuracy and to relieve one another when it all gets a tad too serious – when we can hear the heavy breathing encircle our ears, as clear as the snipping of scissors during a haircut, right before the next killing.

Is any case of murder ever really closed? Certainly those who knew the victim never attain resolution in their hearts or minds. Without even flipping ahead into the journals we haven't yet read, we know there are probably more murders, all linked together like a chain, more victims perhaps all bound together by a common killer, and even more horror for all – yet to come. We know it because we can feel it. Murder is, after all, something you feel forever.

— Hamish De'Lamet & Chandral Ramon Lynchburg, 2009

Who is Emma, and why should you dial her phone number for...murder? Mysterious answers pepper the pages of Book II of The Time Capsule Murders! Will the strange narrator of the diaries or the police solve and stop the murders? The Unknown Narrator becomes more obsessed with a case that the police say is CLOSED: Were the murders an insane fantasy to begin with?

But why does the violence continue?

You will dive even deeper into the soulless soul of American high school life, and the mysteries revealed in *Why Begins With W* become even more terrifying, as your trembling hand reaches for your phone to.... *Dial Emma For Murder*!

HEX HIGH SCHOOL
Our Courses Are Cursed

Book Three of The Time Capsule Murders
Presented by Hamish De'Lamet & Chandral Ramon

Welcome to HEX HIGH SCHOOL! Here students ask themselves: "When will the murders stop?" In Why Begins With W, the first book in The Time Capsule Murders trilogy, a Freshman, trying to solve the mystery of the hidden evil in the school, invited you on a journey into fear itself. In Dial Emma For Murder, the sequel, the journey took you beyond fear and into the reality of terror. Now, to solve the mystery, you must finally follow this Freshman down the hall and into the very heart of a pitiless wasteland known as HEX HIGH SCHOOL!